RAPunzel

A HAPPENIN' RAP

By
David Vozar

Illustrated by
Betsy Lewin

A Picture Yearling Book

Published by
Bantam Doubleday Dell Books for Young Readers
a division of
Random House, Inc.
1540 Broadway
New York, New York 10036

Text copyright © 1998 by David Vozar
Illustrations copyright © 1998 by Betsy Lewin

Visit us on the Web! www.randomhouse.com
Educators and librarians, for a variety of teaching tools, visit us
at www.randomhouse.com/teachers

ISBN: 0-440-41337-0
The text of this book is set in 14.5-point Century Old Style.
Reprinted by arrangement with Doubleday Books for Young Readers
Printed in the United States of America
July 1999
10 9 8 7 6 5 4 3 2

This book is dedicated to family . . .
my mom and pop,
Mark, Amy, Laura, and Sarah,
and my daughter, Ariane.

—D.V.

In memory of L. Frank Baum.
—B.L.

The *Hair-Raising* Beginning

Here's a tale 'bout the girl with long locks,
Lived not far from here, maybe four blocks.
You may think you already know what happened,
But you'll know more after hearing my rapping.

It started when this man and his wife
Were living small in hunger and strife.
They were expecting their first baby to come
When the daddy-to-be did something real dumb.

He went to buy marshmallow ice cream.
Bought a big scoop and in a daydream,
He was thinking up some names for his child
When he bumped into someone outrageously wild.

His ice cream went flying and spilled out.
The guy looked up when he heard a shout.
It was the bad witch from the building next door,
Now covered in goo like a humongous s'more.

The folks in the hood knew she was mean,
The evilest witch they'd ever seen.
And now she was angry, crinkled up her nose,
As the man reached up, started wiping her clothes.

The witch said, "Stop fussing. Tell me now,
Would you like to be a newt or a cow?"
The shocked man said, "I'm sorry! Please don't zap me!
My wife is pregnant. I'll soon be a pappy."

She said, "Off with you! Out of my face!"
The dude ran home as if in some race.
Witch followed behind him 'cause she was still mad,
To snatch his new baby and make him feel bad.

His daughter was born later that day.
The witch appeared and said, "Now you'll pay."
She pointed her wand and *zap!* came a bright light.
"Say good-bye, baby . . . and to all a good night!"

Witch whisked Rapunzel to a building so rare
With one high window, no door and no stairs.
Up, up, went the baby, to the highest room,
Where no one would find her. You'd think she was doomed.

Baby Rapunzel grew up to a girl—
After six years had a full head of curls.

Rapunzel, the girl, grew up to a teen—
Her curls grew faster than you've ever seen.

Rapunzel, the teen, grew up so fair—
But now she had more than ten feet of hair

The Locked-Up Rapunzel

Witch spent all her time pleasing Rap.
All Rap wanted, the witch would just *zap!*
She zapped braces for Rap's crooked molars.
When Rap wanted curls, *Zap!* appeared rollers.

But Rapunzel soon wanted "More! More!"
Whining and whining from noon to four.
She whined for a TV and radio.
She whined to have pizza made to go.

She whined for all the latest teen mags.
A new wardrobe— "My stuff is all rags.
I must have the newest designer wear."
The witch grew tired. Rap didn't care.

One day Witch said, "Enough is enough!
I'm tuckered out from zapping you stuff.
I'm out of here, Toots. You're on your own."
Rap never liked being home alone.

The witch hollered, "Rap, heed my warning.
Better stay alone until the morning.
You know that you belong only to me.
Don't talk to no one. You're mine, you see."

The witch climbed down the stunning girl's locks
As I was jogging right down her block.
They call me Fine Prince. Everyone loves me.
There's no one who rises above me.

I looked up and saw the mean witch there.
Sliding right down some long silky hair.
The witch was yelling, "Rapunzel, see ya!
Be good or I . . . wouldn't wanna be ya!"

Then *poof!* the witch disappeared from sight.
The hair was pulled up to that great height.
I yelled, "Yo! Rapunzel!" and saw her face,
Then knew I had to get in that place.

I sang, "Rapunzel, let down your hair,
'Cause I'm so *fine,* we'd be a great pair."
She said, "Not now, Prince, maybe in a while.
I broke a nail. I've got to file."

I called again after an hour.
Her answer came down from the tower:
"I would love to see you. That's a sure bet.
But I've just shampooed. My hair's all wet."

I waited there but had to get in.
This hot, hot day was bad for my skin.
I heard her blow-dryer, drying away.
I sat and sat for most of the day.

Much later I called, "Drop your hair down."
Again her reply, it made me frown:
"You'll have to wait for a longer while
'Cause my hair's teased in a new def style."

When I saw her hair, "Oh no!" I said.
It shot straight up, way high, on her head.
There's no way that hair could be my ladder.
So, I sat . . . couldn't feel any sadder.

Two hours passed, then I heard the girl:
"This hair is lame. I've had it with curls.
I'll straighten it out, dress it with flowers.
It won't take long, just a few more hours."

I took a short nap there on the stoop,
When I awoke, was thrown for a loop.
There was Rapunzel, the girl of my dreams.
Down dropped her hair, so shiny it gleamed.

Climbing was rough. It took me a bit.
Her shrill whining was giving me fits.
"You're hurting my hair. When it twists and bends,
Your heavy weight will give me split ends."

Finally I made it up to her room.
I fell in love, but then heard a *kaboom!*
The mean witch was back and, man, she looked mad.
Her wand started smoking. This looked bad.

Next thing I knew I was zapped downtown
Where I didn't know my way around.
I was really lost, man. I'm not joking!
Then I pulled out my subway token.

I subwayed back to Rapunzel's place
But she'd disappeared without a trace.
I imagined the worst . . . bad to gory.
What happened next? Yo! Finish my story.

Rapunzel's Brush with Disaster and the Happy Split-Ending

After the witch zapped me out of her face,
She ran to Rapunzel, invaded her space.
She screamed, "I zap things to fill your every whim,
And when I come back, I find you with him!"

The witch got mad, then madder at the girl.
Rapunzel didn't care, sat twirling a curl.
"I'm glad you're back 'cause there's more stuff I need.
Like headphones, some sneakers," Rap said with greed.

Strange things happen when witches get that mad.
Their heads puff up big; that's when things turn real bad.
Rap then spoke again and blew the witch's mind:
"I never get anything!" young Rap whined.

Witch got so angry she overloaded
And all of a sudden her head exploded.
The blast shot dear Rapunzel out the window,
Hair cushioned her fall on the street below.

For weeks I searched the town for my dream girl.
Was wandering around when I noticed a curl.
"It looks like Rapunzel's!" I sang out with glee,
And followed the locks first one block, then three.

The locks led me to a hair-cutting place.
Inside snipped Rapunzel, a smile on her face.
I ran up to her and kissed her cheek so fair.
Then spat on the floor, my mouth filled with hair.

Rapunzel found her parents. That was good.
Then we all settled down, there in the hood.
Rap and I knew one thing—that's how to look fab.
We opened a shop that made beauties from drab.

Rap's hairstyles were a huge sensation.
Everyone had her look across the nation.
Kids, grown-ups, and even some teachers
Were looking cool with Rap's long-hair features.

But that wasn't how we got so happy.
We got all our kicks as a mom and pappy.
When Rapunzel gave birth to two kids, a pair—
A boy and a girl, with six feet of hair.

Rap was happy just styling their tresses,
In cornrows, dread locks, in curls or headdresses.
But out in the hood, Rap got all the stares.
That trendsetting girl had cut off all her hair.

NO-SEW
LOW-SEW

INTERIOR
DECOR

JANIS BULLIS

NO-SEW LOW-SEW

INTERIOR DECOR

Instant style using easy techniques:
gluing, stapling, fusing,
draping, gathering

JANIS BULLIS

krause
publications

A QUARTO BOOK

Copyright © 1996 Quarto Inc.

ISBN 0-8019-8747-4

Reprinted   2002

This book was designed and produced by
Quarto Inc.
The Old Brewery
6 Blundell Street
London N7 9BH

Senior art editor Elizabeth Healey
Designer Tania Field
Senior editor Heather Magrill
Editors Barbara Cheney,
Eleanor Van Zandt
Photographer Paul Forrester
Illustrators Tony Masero, Neil Ballpit,
David McAllister
Picture research manager
Giulia Hetherington
Art director Moira Clinch
Editorial director Mark Dartford

Typeset in Great Britain by
Central Southern Typesetters, Easbourne
Manufactured by Eray Scan Pte Ltd,
Singapore
Printed in China

CONTENTS

INTRODUCTION

WHETHER YOU WISH to completely redecorate your home or simply add a few accessories to one room, you are sure to find inspiration in this book. The projects are quick and easy to make using a combination of simple sewing and non-sewing techniques, exploiting the newest sewing aids on the market.

Step-by-step instructions are given for all of the projects, which can be completed by those with or without sewing experience. Someone already conversant with the craft of sewing can learn about and experiment with the latest in sewing techniques, while a person who is just starting to sew can take advantage of the shortcuts without having to learn the more time-consuming traditional methods.

Choosing fabrics

There are many beautiful fabrics available for home decorating, and it is often these that inspire people to try their hand at sewing. It is easy to fall in love with a particular fabric – seduced, perhaps, by its luscious color, interesting pattern, or cool, crisp texture. But before you select it for a project you should first consider some practical matters.

The two most important considerations in choosing the right fabric are the fiber content and the way it is constructed. The fiber is spun into yarn, and the yarn is made into fabric; how this yarn is woven (or sometimes knitted) will determine how durable the fabric is.

The fiber can be natural – that is, derived from plants or animals; cotton, linen, silk, and wool are natural fibers. Or it can be man-made, or synthetic – that is, produced from chemicals; polyester, nylon, and acetate are synthetic fibers. Each fiber has distinctive qualities, which determine its suitability for different uses. Some of these qualities are negative: cotton, for example, has a reputation for shrinking, acetate for losing its color, and linen for creasing easily. However, it is possible to blend two or more fibers in a fabric, thus counterbalancing their good and bad properties. Alternatively, the manufacturer can apply a finish to the fabric to add body, prevent fading, or discourage wrinkling.

Color, texture, and pattern are all part of the magic of fabric.

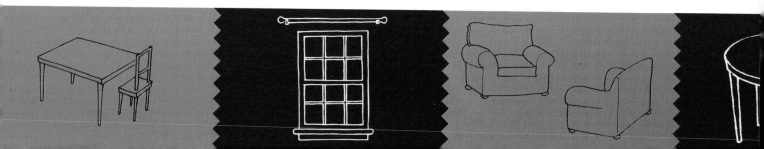

The type of weave will determine the durability of the fabric.

The density of the fabric you choose will depend upon its use.

Decorator fabrics Most decorator fabrics are woven, as this method of construction is more stable than knitting. The type and density of the weave determines the durability of the fabric. For instance, a lightweight fabric made from fine yarns woven densely may well prove to be more durable than a heavy fabric made from loosely woven yarns.

Other fabrics Fabric designed for clothing can be used for some home decorating projects. These fabrics are usually lighter in weight and narrower than decorator fabrics but can be suitable for some informal curtains and accessories.

Sheets and readymade comforter covers can often substitute effectively for decorator fabric, and we have suggested using them in several projects. They are now available in an amazing variety of pretty designs and are economical and easy to care for. In addition, the extra-wide width and readymade hems can cut your sewing time in half.

Variations on a theme: experiment with different styles and materials before making your final choice.

Instructions for caring for the fabric can often be found on the label (if not, ask the salesperson). The amount of wear or dirt to which the finished project will be subjected should be taken into account. For instance, kitchen curtains will need frequent cleaning and should be made of a washable fabric, whereas living-room draperies will need only occasional dry cleaning. The bed covering in a child's bedroom will probably need a wrinkle-resistant and stain-repellent finish, whereas that on a seldom-used guest bed may not.

Fabric amounts In some of the project instructions in this book the required fabric amount has been specified. In others, the amount will depend on your own requirements – for example, on the size of bed or window for which the project is intended. Read through the project instructions first, and draw a plan including the relevant measurements. Take this to the store and use it as a basis for calculating the amount of fabric to buy. Make sure to allow for pattern repeats and possible shrinkage. A calculator is also useful, although the salesperson can usually be called on for help in figuring out the required amount.

There is a wealth of fabric designs to choose from, color and texture can be similar or complementary.

Draped, swagged or stretched over screens, fabric creates atmosphere. Choose accessories to match or to contrast.

"Sewing" without thread The latest inventions in sewing technology include products that have little to do with a needle and thread. It is now possible to join two pieces of fabric by gluing or fusing them together. Such materials as interfacing, quilt batting, and drapery tapes can also often be applied with adhesives rather than by sewing.

Once you have learned the techniques and become familiar with the use of these products through the projects in this book, you can go on to experiment with using them in other projects. By all means, make use of the basic sewing techniques where appropriate, but don't be afraid to break with tradition.

Whatever the project, try to approach it in a pragmatic, innovative spirit. If it makes sense to fuse, rather than stitch, the hems of your curtains – why not? If a sheet has the perfect color and pattern for your kitchen, make it into some quilted placemats and matching napkins. Turn an exquisite dresser scarf into a pillow cover. You may be surprised at how much fun sewing (and non-sewing!) can be.

Contrasting patterns can produce luxurious effects.

Curtain rings come in various styles and materials. Choose to suit the effect you want.

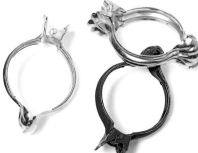

BEFORE YOU BEGIN

Each project includes a list of basic techniques required to complete it. All of these techniques are described here. You should first read through this section to familiarize yourself with the equipment and techniques; then, when making a specific project, you can refer to a certain technique if necessary. In every case we have chosen the techniques that are most conducive to an accurate and easy assembly of the project.

MEASURING UP

It is important that your measurements be full and accurate. All the measurements you need for the projects in this book are included here.

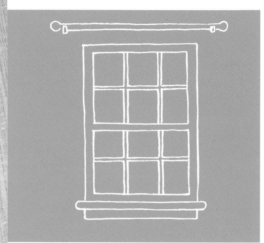

WINDOWS

For the best results when making curtains, draperies, or other window treatments, you should fix the rod or mounting board first, before calculating fabric amounts. This will enable you to cut and hem panels accurately.

Measuring the width To purchase the appropriate length of rod or mounting board, you must first decide whether the draperies or shade, for example, should be fixed inside or outside the window frame. For an inside mount, measure between the inside edges of the window frame. An inside mount may not be possible for windows positioned more or less flush with the wall.

For an outside mount, attach the brackets to the wall, rather than to the window frame. It may be desirable to use a rod long enough so that the draperies, when open, will stack back on the wall to expose all of the glass. Measure the desired distance to each side from the outside of the window frame – anywhere from 2″ to 18″ may be required.

Measure the length of the mounted rod, then determine the required fullness of the fabric. Depending upon the project, the finished fabric width can be equal to the rod length (as in the case of a roller

shade, for example) or up to three times the length (for full glass curtains, for example). The fullness is often expressed as a ratio for example, a ratio of 2:1 means that the curtain or drapery is twice the width of the window.

Measuring the length Mount the rod or board 1″ to 4″ above the top edge of the window frame. Measure the distance from the top of the rod or mounting board to the desired position of the lower edge of the window treatment: at the sill, below the apron, or to the floor. The calculations for each project take into consideration casings (which fit over the rod), headings, and hems. All floor-length draperies finish ½″ above the floor.

Installing window treatments The construction of the wall or window frame will determine the type of hardware needed to mount a drapery/curtain rod or mounting board brackets. Be sure to anchor the rod or board securely for heavy draperies or a treatment to which extra strain will be applied when raising and lowering.

After the rod or board is mounted, measure its length between the brackets. Also, using a tape measure, measure the circumference of a curtain rod for a casing. You should normally allow a little extra to this measurement when calculating the size of the casing, so that the fabric will glide smoothly over the rod. To test the effect, cut a strip of fabric to the estimated size of the casing and slip it over the rod. Additional fabric should be allowed for the heading above the casing.

A mounting board can be used either inside or outside the window frame. To camouflage the board, you can paint it a color similar to the fabric or wrap the entire board in fabric, depending upon how much of the board will be visible. Mount it with L brackets to the molding for an inside mount or to the wall for an outside mount.

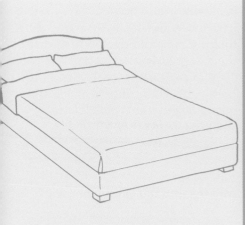

BEDS

Although most beds are manufactured in standard sizes, it is best to measure the bed itself to be sure of accuracy. Measure the width and length of the bed across the mattress.

Measure the thickness of the mattress. Measure the height of the box spring from the floor and the height of the mattress from the floor. The finished size of the project can be determined from these measurements.

Standard American mattress sizes		Standard American bed pillow sizes	
Twin	39″ × 75″	Standard	20″ × 26″
Full	54″ × 75″	Queen	20″ × 30″
Queen	60″ × 80″	King	20″ × 38″
King	78″ × 80″		

PILLOWS

Bed pillows are also available in standard sizes, but because of the wide variety in the methods of construction, it is best to measure the pillow from seam to seam. Measure throw pillows in the same way.

CHAIRS

When measuring an armchair or sofa, it is important to remember to be generous with the measurements. A little bit of fabric is used up every time it dips around a seat or cushion or rolls over an arm. Pinning or basting the seams before they are sewn will help to customize the fit.

Dining chairs For square or rectangular seats, measure the length and width of the seat. For those chair seats that narrow toward the back or are a unique shape, place paper over the seat and trace the shape. Measure the depth and perimeter of the seat cushion. Add seam and hem allowances where necessary.

Sofas and armchairs Measure the width of the sofa from the floor in front, up to the seat, across the seat to the back, up the back and down again to the floor in back of the sofa. Measure the length of the sofa from the floor at one side, up over the shoulder, across the back, over the other shoulder and down to the floor again. Be generous, not conservative, with these measurements as any excess fabric can be tucked into the gap of the chair between the seat cushion and inside arm. For the armchair, take these same width and length measurements with the cushion removed; measure the width, length and depth of the cushion separately. Piece together panels of fabric and add seam and hem allowances where necessary.

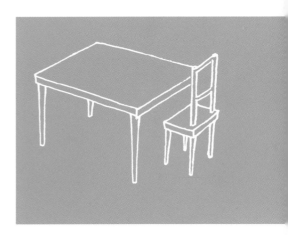

TABLES

Measure the width and length or the diameter of the table top. Measure the height of the table from the edge to the floor or to the seat of the chair.

JOINING FABRIC WIDTHS

A single fabric width is often narrower than the width of the item you are making. The number of widths needed, the method of cutting and joining them, and the necessity of matching a printed or woven design all need to be considered at the outset.

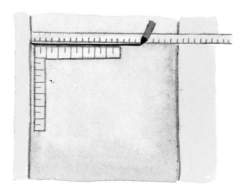

Grain This is the direction of the threads in a woven fabric. The lengthwise grain of the fabric runs parallel to the selvage, or finished edge. The crosswise grain runs at a right angle to it. If the fabric needs to be cut along the lengthwise grain, measure the required distance from the selvage at two or more points, mark these points, and join them to make a line parallel to the selvage. If the fabric is to be cut along the crosswise grain, line up one leg of a carpenter's square along the selvage; the adjacent leg will follow the crosswise grain.

Before buying fabric, make sure that the two grains run correctly at right angles to each other. Most

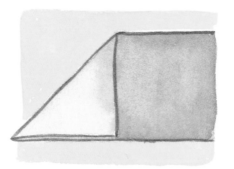

good-quality decorator fabrics do, but if the cut edge shows the crosswise threads running diagonally to the selvage, it is probably unwise to buy it.

Bias This refers to the 45-degree angle that runs between the lengthwise and crosswise grains. To find the bias, fold the fabric so that the two grains are aligned.

Woven fabric is stable along both grain lines, without much give; but when it is pulled along the bias, it stretches. Cut fabric along the bias when extra stretch is needed – for example, to make bias tape or strips to cover cord. Also see *Making and applying trimmings.*

Directional fabrics If the fabric has a one-way design (one that looks different when viewed from the two ends) or a nap (a raised surface), pieces should be cut and joined so that the design or nap runs in the same direction, where appropriate. When making draperies, for example, mark the top of each fabric width before joining the widths. It is easy enough to determine the direction on some fabrics – e.g. one printed with standing birds; a piece with the birds upside down would be readily apparent. Less obvious are busy florals, geometrics, asymmetrical stripes, some plaids, and fabrics with a nap. To avoid confusion, mark lengths of directional fabric with tape or a safety pin at the top as they are cut.

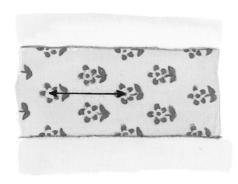

Repeats The design of a printed, striped, or plaid fabric repeats at regular intervals. The length of this repeat should be taken into consideration before purchasing and cutting, as described below. In most cases the repeat distance is given on the label. If it is not, measure from the center of a prominent motif, along the lengthwise grain to the center of the next identical motif. Make a note of the measurement.

Matching the pattern When joining pieces of patterned fabric, you will need to match the pattern repeat at the seams. Regardless of the fabric width, a quality decorator fabric is designed so that the pattern can be matched at the seams with no unsightly break in the print, even when several widths are

sewn together.

You will probably have enough fabric to be able not only to match the design but also to take full seam allowances and trim away and discard the selvages. Some fabric at the top or bottom of each piece must often be wasted in order to match the design. In order to be sure you are purchasing enough fabric, add the repeat measurement to every length you need. For a large design repeat you may need to add as much as ¾yd for every length needed. At first, the extra expenditure may seem unnecessary and wasteful, but the importance of cutting the pieces in this way will soon become evident.

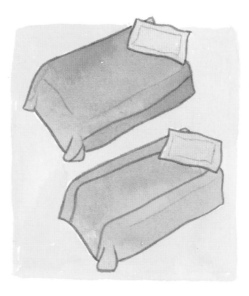

Balancing The finished width of the project will determine how many fabric lengths will be needed. Their positioning should be planned carefully. As a general rule, whole fabric widths should be placed at the

center of a project and partial widths at the sides, to avoid center seams. Any partial widths must be equal to ensure symmetry. This balancing is equally important for solid-colored fabric with no design repeat.

For a one-piece project, such as a comforter cover, allow a whole width at the center and split one or trim from two whole widths at the sides.

For a two-piece project, such as a pair of draperies, place a whole width at the inner edge of each panel and a partial width (if necessary) at the outer edges.

For some projects, a whole width at the center may be too wide. This often happens with bed covers when only a narrow strip is necessary on each side to make up the full width, resulting in seams very near the edges – a clear indication of their piecing function. To make the seams appear part of the project's design, trim some fabric from the sides of the center piece and cut the side pieces correspondingly wider.

If the fabric has a printed or woven pattern, you will need to experiment – before cutting the project to size – to match the pattern at the seams. Allow a whole extra repeat when cutting the center piece and do not trim it at the sides. Then move the side pieces along it at the chosen positions for the seams until the pattern matches. Then seam the sections together and trim the center piece as required.

Making patterns and cutting shapes

Home decorating projects seldom require a paper pattern. They normally consist of simple shapes, such as rectangles or circles, which can be marked directly on the fabric. However, you may find it convenient sometimes to make a paper pattern first – if, for example, a shape is relatively complex or if several identical fabric pieces must be cut, in which case marking them individually would entail extra work. Simply mark the shapes on the paper as specified in the project instructions. Add seam allowances where necessary. Pin the pattern to the fabric and cut around it.

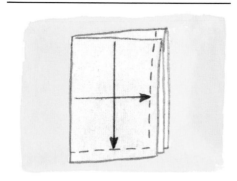

Rectangles and squares It is imperative for squares and rectangles to have all adjacent sides at right angles to each other. To achieve a right angle, place a carpenter's square or right-angled triangle along the lengthwise grain of the fabric and then measure the desired width and length from each of the legs of the square.

Due to the size of some projects, it is sometimes difficult to measure and cut accurately – even the floor may not be big enough. In such a case, the solution is to cut pieces slightly longer and wider than required, join the seams, then trim the edges as follows. Fold the seamed fabric in half widthwise and then in half again lengthwise, keeping all the cut edges even. Measuring from the two adjacent folded edges, determine the cutting size by dividing each dimension – length and width – in half. (Remember to add outer seam/hem allowance.) This method requires less space and with careful measurements can be just as accurate.

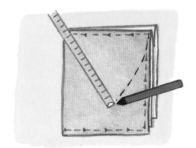

Circles For circular patterns, begin with a square cut to the diameter of the circle, including seam/hem allowance. Fold the fabric in half twice, matching all cut edges. Pin the layers together at the edges. Divide the diameter by 2 to get the radius. Using a tape measure as a compass, measure and mark the radius from the folded corner at frequent intervals. (Place a heavy object at the corner to hold the tape in place for each mark.) Join the marks in a curved line, then cut through all the layers along this line. Unfold the fabric for a perfect circle.

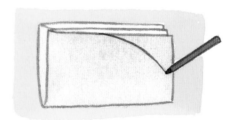

Ovals For oval patterns, begin with a rectangle cut to the desired outer dimensions. Fold the fabric in half lengthwise and in half again crosswise, matching all cut edges. Locate the open corner (without folds) and, measuring the two adjacent sides, mark a curved line along it. (You may wish to make a paper pattern for this to ensure a smooth, well-proportioned curve.) Cut through all the layers along the marked line.

Braid, cord, bias tape, lace, and ribbon are all readily available in hundreds of styles and colors to give a finishing touch to your decorating project. With a little more investment in time, you can make your own trim from fabric. Bias tape is made from narrow strips of fabric cut on the bias; these can also be used to cover a filler cord to make piping. Stitch the strips together following the fabric grain to achieve the length needed.

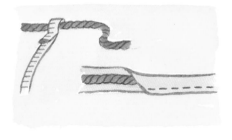

Piping To make piping, first measure the circumference of the piping cord and add seam allowances. The total is the cutting width of the strips. Fold the strips

around the cord and stitch close to the cord, using the zipper foot on the machine.

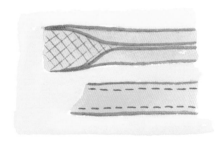

Single-fold bias tape To make a single-fold bias tape, allow twice the finished width when cutting. Place the strip wrong side up on the ironing board, and turn in the edges so that they meet in the center; press. Stitch the tape flat to the project along each fold.

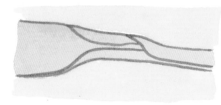

Double-fold bias tape To make double-fold bias tape, allow four times the finished width. Press the strip lengthwise, as for single-fold tape, with the cut edges meeting in the center. Then fold the strip in half down the center, enclosing the cut edges. The tape is applied to the edge of the fabric as a practical seam finish or decorative trimming.

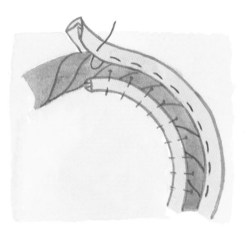

Applying tape To apply the tape to curves, stretch the outer edges slightly and shrink the inner edge with steam from an iron, easing it around the curve. Hold the tape in place with plenty of pins, or basting, then stitch flat.

To miter a corner, when applying a single-fold tape, first stitch the tape to the position of the corner along both edges; then break the stitching and fold the tape diagonally to form a right angle. Resume stitching along the adjacent edges.

To miter double-fold tape when binding an edge, stitch through all layers up to the corner, and break off the stitching. Fold the tape back on itself on the front and the back. Pin the folds in place securely, then resume stitching.

GENERAL SEWING EQUIPMENT

All the equipment necessary to complete the projects is listed here. You can easily buy any of the items in your local sewing or department store.

Tape measure A flexible tape measure that will not stretch is an essential tool.

Spring-return metal tape This extra-long tape measure is helpful for large projects.

Yardstick A good non-flexible measuring tool which is also useful for marking straight edges.

Carpenter's square or **right-angled triangle** Either of these can be used to measure right angles; some triangles will also measure 45-degree angles.

Seam gauge A small ruler with a sliding marker is helpful when marking small distances, as for seams and hems.

Magnetic seam guide
A sewing machine attachment to ensure a uniform and accurate seam width. It is easily adjusted for sewing wider headings and hems.

MARKING EQUIPMENT

Fabric-marking pencil Also known as a quilter's pencil, this is a readily visible and easy-to-remove method of marking fabric. A few colors will suffice for all fabrics.

Marking chalk
A temporary marking method suitable for some fabrics. Chalk is available in pencil form, by a quilter's pencil, this is a readily visible and easy-to-remove method of marking fabric. A few colors will suffice for all fabrics.

Air-soluble pen A pen filled with ink that evaporates after a period of time. It is ideal for temporary markings.

Water-soluble pen A pen filled with ink that can be removed with a damp cloth. It is good to use on washable fabrics and for markings that need to remain over the course of a few days or weeks.

Tracing wheel and paper Useful for transferring pattern markings to fabric. The marks may be permanent or temporary, depending on the brand.

Note Before using any marking material, test it on a scrap of the fabric.

CUTTING EQUIPMENT

Dressmakers' shears These long-bladed scissors have handles shaped to fit the hand, with openings for a thumb on one side and for several fingers on the other. The angle between blades and handles makes them ideal for cutting fabric placed flat on a table.

Sewing scissors These are useful for trimming seam allowances, clipping curves, and many other jobs.

Pinking shears One of the fastest methods of clean finishing a seam to prevent raveling. Because of the variation in width that they produce, they are not intended for cutting out the fabric.

Seam ripper Used for safely removing stitching mistakes and machine basting stitches. Available in large and small sizes.

Hand and machine needles Choose the size and type according to the fiber content and number of layers of fabric. Choose sewing thread following the same guidelines.

Thimble Protects the middle fingertip when hand sewing; especially useful when sewing thick fabrics.

Iron For pressing wrinkles from fabric, pressing seams, creasing fold and hems, and applying most fusible webs and interfacing.

Bodkin These come in different styles, including one resembling tweezers with locking teeth. It grabs the end of a length of elastic or ribbon and is then used to pull it through a stitched casing. A large safety pin can serve the same purpose.

• 30 Assorted Needles •

Seam roll Originally designed for tailoring, this tool is helpful in home decorating projects for pressing seams. It is inserted in tubular shapes and placed on the ironing board; the seam can then be pressed without creasing the fabric.

Quilter's clips These large spring-form rings hold a rolled-up section of a quilt, making the opposite end easier to work on and the size of the project more manageable.

Pins Extra-long pins, especially those with large ball or T-shaped heads, are the best choice for heavier home decorating fabrics.

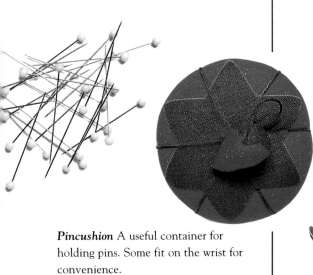

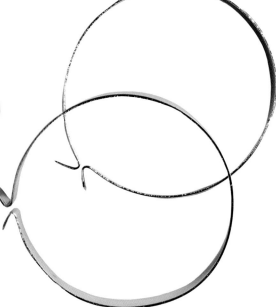

Pincushion A useful container for holding pins. Some fit on the wrist for convenience.

FUSING MATERIALS

Seam sealant A liquid applied to the cut edge of woven fabric to prevent raveling.

Permanent adhesive A liquid white glue designed specifically for fabric.

Fusible web strips Fabric adhesive that resembles a strip of netting. It is used to bond two layers of fabric together, or fabric to a porous surface such as cardboard. The adhesive melts when heat from an iron is applied to the fabric. It is available in several widths, as a permanent or temporary adhesive, and with or without a paper backing.

Glue stick This adhesive is useful for holding edges together before they are stitched, and so serves the same purpose as basting. It will wash out.

Fusible web sheets Similar to fusible web strips but much wider.

FILLERS

Quilt batting The filler between two layers of fabric in a quilt or comforter. It is available in many thicknesses and sizes, and also as a fusible product.

Pillow forms Preformed shapes of polyurethane or fiber-filled fabric are available in several sizes and geometric shapes. Feather-filled pillow forms can be obtained through some specialty suppliers.

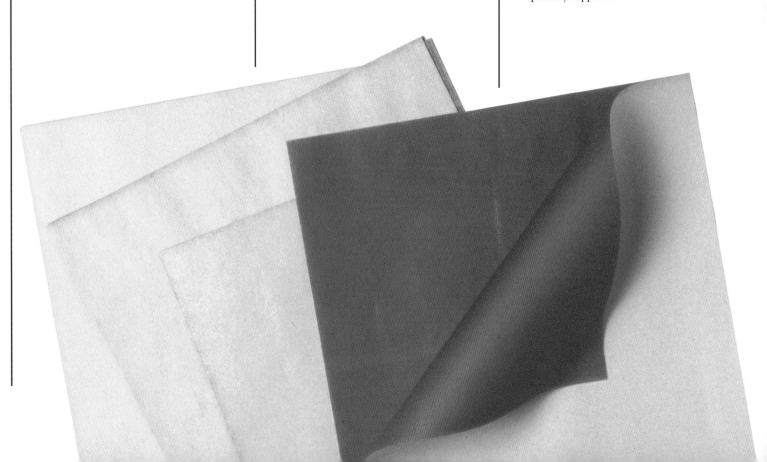

BASIC STITCHING TECHNIQUES

The various stitches used in the projects are very simple, but it is important to use the right stitch for the right purpose. All the stitches and their uses are described here.

The large size and the long straight lines of most home decorating projects dictate that almost all of the seaming, hemming, and finishing be sewn by machine, rather than by hand. It is also this simplicity of design that makes these projects ideal for fusing and gluing materials. Before you decide whether to stitch or fuse a project, or part of a project, together, see **When to sew and when to fuse.**

Straight stitching This stitch, which forms a thin, solid line, is the one you will normally use, especially for seams. Unless otherwise instructed, you should allow ½in seam allowance throughout. Once stitched, the seam should be pressed open, even if it will later be pressed to one side. This initial pressing helps to embed the stitches in the fabric and give a crisp finish. In some cases you will need to trim the seam allowance to reduce bulk. Also clip the excess from corners and curved seams.

Zigzag stitching A line of zigzag stitch is an ideal way to clean-finish seam allowances. Worked close to the raw edge, the stitches will prevent the fabric from continuing to ravel. (Some fabrics do not require clean finishing, and it is not necessary for items that are fully lined.) A zigzag stitch is also used to stitch appliqués by machine. For a dense stitch that covers the edges of the motif completely – called satin stitch – set the stitch as short and as wide as possible.

Buttons, traditionally sewn on by hand, are easily sewn by machine on a zigzag setting with the feed dog (teeth) of the machine disengaged. See your machine instruction manual for details.

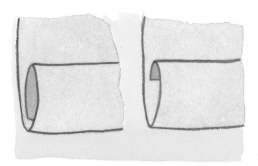

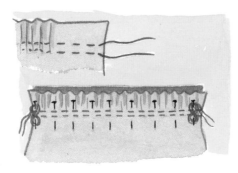

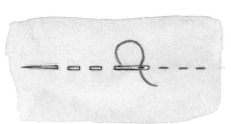

Hemming Unless otherwise instructed, always plan for a double hem in home decorating projects. Besides giving the project a professional-looking finish, this helps to give the fabric weight and therefore more drapability – especially desirable in curtains and draperies. It also makes the hem appear more uniform. Choose a single hem when you need to minimize bulk or when an applied trimming will provide the necessary weight.

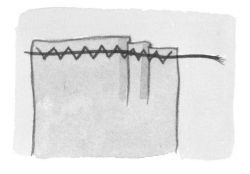

Gathering over cord For a slightly stronger gathering method, zigzag over a lightweight cord placed within the seam allowance. Pull the cord to gather the fabric.

Gathering with machine basting
A long straight machine stitch is one way of gathering fabric for ruffles. You can either work one row within the seam allowance, or two rows straddling the seamline. When the stitching is complete, pull up the bobbin thread to form the gathering. Secure the thread ends around pins, then adjust the gathers evenly and pin the ruffle in place.

Because most decorator fabrics are relatively heavy, and gathering may need to be worked over long distances, placing a strain on the stitching, it is a good idea to use a heavy-duty thread for this purpose. Wind the heavy thread on the bobbin and use ordinary thread for the needle. When you come to pull the bobbin thread to gather the fabric, it is less likely to break.

Machine basting A long straight stitch, this helps to hold fabrics, interfacings, or trimmings in place until the permanent stitching can be done. Some machines will do an extra-long stitch, ½in long, for this purpose.

Basting by hand When joining fabric layers temporarily, it is sometimes easiest to use a long running stitch, instead of pins, which can slip out, or machine basting, which is impractical if the item is very unwieldy.

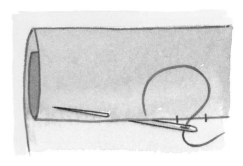

Slipstitch This stitch is used where it is not possible to use the machine and where fabrics and/or trims need to be joined invisibly. The needle catches a few fabric threads of one layer, then goes through the adjacent folded edge (or simply under a finished edge, as in braid, for example) and up, then back into the other fabric layer.

When to sew and when to fuse

The straight seams and hems found in home decorating projects are ideal for using the fusible materials and fabric glues on the market.

Fusible web

The best choice for turning up hems is narrow strips of fusible web, usually sold on rolls. Some of these strips have a paper backing, which makes application a two-step process; this allows for greater accuracy.

The great advantage of hemming with fusible web is that no stitches show on the right side. Using web strips to apply ribbon helps to keep it flat and wrinkle free. The strips can even be used for seaming, provided that no stress will be applied to the seam.

Fusible web is also available in wide sheets. Web with temporary adhesive is excellent for holding the edges of an intricate appliqué motif in place until it is sewn. Web with permanent adhesive can be used to bond layers without the need for sewing, even if the item is to be laundered many times.

Fusing fabrics

Each manufacturer of fusible web provides specific instructions for applying their product, and these can differ greatly from one manufacturer to the next, even for the same type of web. All webs are applied with an ordinary household iron; the major difference lies in whether or not the manufacturer recommends the use of steam. Those with a removable paper backing may require a dry iron for the first stage and a steam iron after the paper is removed. Other differences include the temperature setting and the amount of time and pressure needed. For the best results, always follow the manufacturer's instructions carefully, and test the web on a scrap of fabric to see how the two react.

Fabric glue

Fabric glue is permanent and strong and best used in small areas, especially those that will receive added stress. Use it, for example, to hold the corner of a seam that may be subjected to strain. It is also useful for applying bulky trimming that may be difficult to sew. Look for glue that

  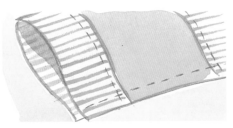

remains soft and pliable while you are working with it and that will not bleed through or discolor the fabric.

A liquid seam sealant is the chemical way to clean-finish cut edges. It bonds the fibers together to prevent the cut edge of the fabric from raveling, yet without impairing the fabric's soft texture.

Quilt batting and interfacing

The purpose of interfacing is to add body to a fabric – a job that fusible interfacing does very well, provided the area is not too large, in which case the interfacing may be difficult to apply smoothly. It is ideal along the heading or hem of a drapery panel and on accessories. Fusible quilt batting, too, is best used in small items, such as crib quilts, and placemats.

Drapery construction tape

The newest product to be offered in fusible form is drapery construction tape. This has pre-measured folds and stitched-in cords and pockets, which allow the tape to be stitched or fused in place while flat. The fabric can then be pleated by drawing the cords. The tape is applied with an iron and then allowed to cool; it is then reheated to make the cords easier to draw or to ease the insertion of the drapery hooks.

When to sew

The fusible products described above are generally marketed as convenient, time-saving alternatives to sewing. Although this is true in many cases, in others it is quicker and easier to sew than to fuse. For instance, if a seam does not lie flat on the ironing board, attempting to fuse it can be a tricky operation. Also, if a seam or hem is very long, you may find that continually positioning the web and fusing it in place over short stretches can become very tedious and time consuming. With experience you'll learn when it makes sense to use the sewing machine.

1 Fusible web: for hems and appliqué.
2 Fabric glue: for small areas, or areas of added strain.
3 Quilt interfacing: adds body to the fabric.
4 Drapery construction tape: can be stitched or fused in place while flat.
5 Sewing: sometimes it is quicker and easier to sew than to fuse.

EASY LIVING

Table top accessories are the perfect answer to quick and easy decorating and in many cases require only a small amount of fabric. Choose them for a special occasion or when you want to make an ordinary day seem special. Window valances, whether ruffled or flat require only a small amount of fabric to soften and add color to an angular frame. Also in this chapter you'll find an alternative to time-consuming tailored slip covers – wrap and tie casual slip covers – appealing and easy to make.

TABLE ACCESSORIES

Combine the simplicity of linen with the delicacy of lace to create an elegant table ensemble.

CHECKLIST

Materials

(for one runner, one placemat, one napkin)
1½yd of 45in-wide linen fabric
¾yd of 45in-wide iron-on interfacing
7yd of 1¼in-wide flat lace trim
3 heart-shaped lace doilies, 10in wide
1 round lace doily, 4in in diameter
General sewing equipment
Liquid seam sealant
Paper for pattern

Techniques

Machine stitching	pp. 22–23
Hand stitching	pp. 22–23
Applying trimmings	pp. 16–17

Making the patterns

Placemat From the pattern paper, measure and cut a rectangle 13 x 19in.
Napkin Measure and cut a square 18 x 18in.
Runner Measure and cut a rectangle 13 x 44in. Measure and mark the center point on each short edge, then mark 7in in from the end of each long side. Cut along these lines to form two points.
Cutting sizes include ½in seam allowance.

1 Using the pattern pieces, cut two placemats, two runners, and one napkin from the fabric. Cut one placemat and one runner from the interfacing. Trim ½in from the edges of the interfacing pieces.

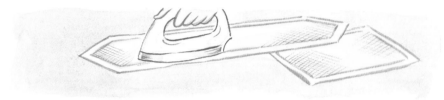

2 Following the manufacturer's instructions, carefully fuse each piece of interfacing to the wrong side of one corresponding fabric piece.

3 Place the two placemat pieces together with right sides facing and edges even. Pin and then stitch them together, leaving a 6in opening along one long edge.

5 Pin the heart doily to the center of the placemat. Topstitch the doily in place around the edge. If the edge is intricate, secure the points with fabric glue.

6 Starting in the center of the lower edge, pin the lace trim around the edge of the placemat on the right side. Lap the straight edge of the lace over the fabric edge. Stitch it in place with two lines of topstitching, turning under the finishing end to conceal the starting end. Topstitch the corners along the fold.

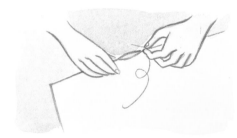

4 Trim the seams and cut across the corners. Press, and turn right side out. Slipstitch the opening edges together and press the placemat flat.

To complete the table runner:

7 Follow the placemat steps 2–5, substituting two heart doilies at each end for the one in the center.

To complete the napkin:

8 Turn under and press ½in on all four edges. Tuck the cut edge in to meet the fold, and press again. Topstitch the double hem along the inside fold.

9 Pin the doily to one corner of the napkin so that it overlaps the edges attractively. Topstitch the doily edges in place, using either zigzag stitch or two rows of straight stitching; take the threads to the wrong side and knot them together securely. Trim away the fabric from under the doily along the stitching line. For added security, apply a liquid seam sealant to prevent fraying of the cut edge.

To make this an even simpler two-seam project, use fusible web for all of the hemming in steps 2–4.

BORDERED CLOTH

Brighten up your next buffet dinner with a bordered tablecloth and matching napkins.

C H E C K L I S T

Materials

2 coordinating decorator fabrics, one with stripes
General sewing equipment
Paper-backed ⅜in-wide fusible web strip

Techniques

Measuring up: tables	pp. 12–13
Joining fabric widths	pp. 14–15
Machine stitching	pp. 12–13
Fusing fabric	pp. 24–25

Measuring up

Measure the width and length of the table. Measure the drop from the edge of the table to the top of the chair seat.

Cutting sizes

Cloth For the cutting width, multiply the drop by 2, then add the table width plus 1in. For the cutting length, multiply the drop by 2, then add the table length plus 1in.
Borders For the cutting width, select a section of the striped fabric measuring approximately 3–4in; measure it and add 1in. The cutting length of each border is equal to the cutting width and length of the cloth.
Napkin Cut these 16in square.
Piece widths of fabric together if necessary to achieve the dimensions of the tablecloth. Cutting sizes include ½in hem allowance.

1 Following the cutting dimensions, cut one cloth from the main decorator fabric and two short borders and two long borders from the striped fabric. Cut one square from the striped fabric for each napkin.

2 On one long edge of each border piece, turn under and press ½in.

3 Pin a short border to a long border, placing right sides together and matching cut ends and folded edges.

4 Keeping the pinned ends even, lift the top border and position it at right angles to the bottom border. Press the diagonal fold.

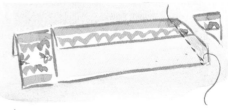

5 Pin and stitch the borders together along the crease of the diagonal fold, backstitching at the ends to secure. Trim the seam ¼in from the stitching.

6 Press the seam. Repeat steps 3–5 to join the other two borders, making sure to join them in the correct order.

7 Following the manufacturer's instructions, apply fusible web to the folded hem allowance on the inner edge of the border. Do not remove the paper backing.

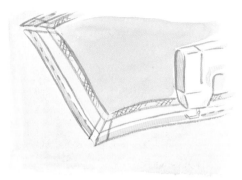

To finish each napkin:

11▶ Turn under and press ½in on all edges of the napkin. Tuck the cut edge in to meet the fold, and press again. Topstitch the double hem along the inside fold, or secure it with fusible web.

8▲ Place the border, right side down, on the wrong side of the cloth with cut edges even. Pin the border to the cloth along the outer edges. Stitch together, taking ½in seam allowance. Trim the seam and clip diagonally across the corners.

10▲ Remove the paper backing and fuse the border to the cloth. Topstitch through all the layers close to the inner edge of the border.

The cloth is hemmed and the border applied in the same step. Perfectly mitered corners are easy to achieve with a simple fold, press, and stitch method, which eliminates calculations and guesswork. This design is for a rectangular or square table.

9▶ Press the seam open, reaching as far into the corners as possible, then turn the border to the right side of the cloth. Push out the corners to make them sharp, and along the outer edge.

TABLECLOTH AND TOPPER

Perfect for the kitchen or patio, this coordinating tablecloth and geranium-print topper add color to the room.

C H E C K L I S T

Materials

2 coordinating decorator fabrics
General sewing equipment
Fusible web strip, ⅛in wide
Fusible cord shirring tape

Techniques

Measuring up: tables	pp. 12–13
Joining fabric widths	pp. 14–15
Cutting the shapes: circles	pp. 16–17
Machine stitching	pp. 22–23

Measuring up

Measure the height of the table and the diameter of the table top.

Cutting sizes

Tablecloth For the cutting width, add twice the table height to the table diameter; add 2in. Piece several widths of fabric together if necessary to achieve the correct width. The cutting length is identical to the width.
Table topper For the cutting width, divide the height by 1.5; add the diameter plus 2in. The cutting length is identical to the width. The cutting dimensions allow the finished tablecloth to clear the floor by ½in. The topper will overhang the table by one-third the height.

1 Following the measurements obtained, cut the larger square from the tablecloth fabric and the smaller one from the topper fabric.

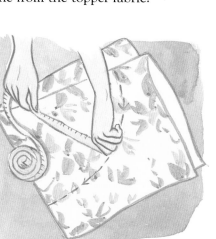

To complete the tablecloth:

2 Fold the cloth in half crosswise and in half again lengthwise. Measure off half the cutting width; this is the radius of the circle. Place the end of the tape measure at the folded corner. Using the tape as a compass, mark a quarter circle on the cloth. Cut along this line through all layers.

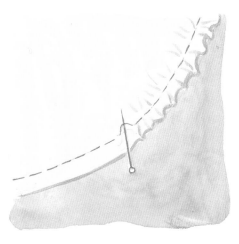

3 Open the folded cloth. Machine baste ¼in from the edge. Approximately every 6in, insert a pin under a basting stitch and gently lift until the fabric gathers slightly.

4 Turn under and press 1in around the edge. Relax or tighten the basting stitches as required for evenly distributed fullness. Tuck the cut edge in to meet the fold, and press again, hiding the basting stitches. Following the manufacturer's instructions, use the fusible web strip to fuse the double hem in place.

To complete the table topper:

▶ 5 Repeat steps 2–4 to cut and hem the topper circle.

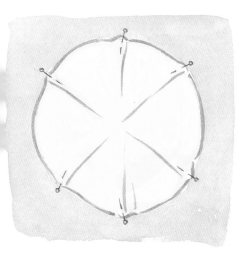

🔺 6 Fold the topper in half, then fold it again into thirds. Mark the edges with pins at the folds. On the wrong side of the fabric, use a yardstick and marking pen to draw three lines between opposite points, thus dividing the circle into six equal segments.

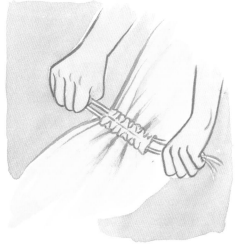

🔺 7 Cut six pieces of shirring tape, each equal to a third of the table height. Position the end of one tape at the hemline and center it on a marked line; fuse the tape in place. Repeat with the other pieces of tape. To gather the topper, pull the cords and tie them together.

Fusing web and an iron are all you need for quick and easy hems if the material you are using has not been finished on all edges.

Appliqued Picnic Basket

When fusible web is used, appliqués of any shape are quick and easy.

CHECKLIST

Materials

Coordinating decorator fabrics
⅜in-wide filler cord
Picnic basket
Poster board
Lightweight quilt batting
Paper-backed fusible web
Fabric glue
General sewing equipment

Techniques

Making patterns and cutting shapes	pp. 16–17
Machine stitching	pp. 22–23
Applying trimmings	pp. 16–17
Fusing fabric	pp. 24–25

Measuring up

Measure the width, length, and perimeter of the picnic basket lid.

Cutting sizes

Fabric Cover For the cutting dimensions, add 3in to the measured length and width.
Piping Strip The cutting width is 2in. The length is the same as the perimeter of the lid plus about 2in. Piece several fabric widths together, if necessary.
Quilt Batting and Poster Board For the cutting dimensions, trace the lid of the basket.
Fruit and Fusible Web For the cutting dimensions, cut a rectangle approximately ½in greater on all edges than each appliqué motif.

1▶ Following the cutting dimensions, cut one fabric cover, one piping strip, one quilt batting piece and one poster board piece.

2▶ Using either pins or an erasable pen, mark the outline of the poster board on the right side of the fabric cover to create an appliqué guideline.

3▶ Place each piece of fusible web, paper side up, on an appliqué motif. Trace the motif using a fairly dark pen. Following the manufacturer's instructions, fuse the web tracing to the wrong side of the appliqué fabric. Cut out the shape.

4▶ Position the appliqués on the right side of the cover, within the guideline. Remove the paper backing from each motif in turn, and fuse it to the fabric.

5▶ Glue the quilt batting to the poster board.

6▶ Lay the cover wrong side up, and center the board, batting side down, on top. Wrap all the edges of the fabric to the back of the board, and glue in place, pleating the fabric at the corners to fit.

7▶ Wrap the strip of piping fabric around the filler cord, with wrong sides facing and edges matching. Using the zipper foot on the sewing machine, stitch close to the cord.

end and the uncovered end of the cord so that they butt together. Turn under ½in on the edge of the overlapping fabric, and wrap the fabric around the join. Pin the ends together. (See Piped Bed Set, step 5, for an illustration of this technique.)

8 Glue the piping to the back of the board around the edges, so that the cord extends over the edge and the ends overlap slightly. Using a needle or sharp-pointed scissors, remove the stitches to approximately 1½in from one end of the piping, and fold back the fabric. Trim the covered

9 Glue the covered board to the top of the picnic basket.

SILVER SERVER

Add beauty to a buffet
dinner with a lace-trimmed
silver server.

CHECKLIST

Materials

⅝yd of 45in-wide decorator fabric
⅝yd of 45in-wide iron-on interfacing
2yd of 1¼in-wide flat lace trim
1 round lace doily, 10in in diameter
½yd of ⅜in-wide ribbon
General sewing equipment
Paper for pattern

Techniques

Making patterns and cutting shapes	pp. 16–17
Machine stitching	pp. 22–23
Hand stitching	pp. 22–23
Applying trimmings	pp. 16–17

Making the pattern

Measure and cut a 20in-diameter circle from
the pattern paper.
Using a pencil and ruler, divide it into 12
equal segments.
Pattern size includes ½in seam allowance.

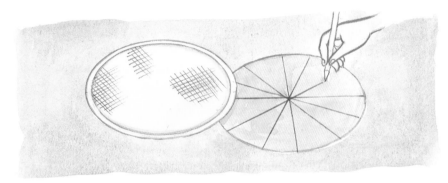

1 Using the pattern piece, cut two circles each from the fabric and interfacing. Trim ½in seam allowance from the edge of the interfacing. Mark the edge of one fabric circle with the segment divisions from the pattern. Then use a ruler and erasable pen, on the right side, to connect these marks with straight lines. Following the manufacturer's instructions, fuse the interfacing to the wrong side of each circle.

2 Pin the lace trim to the right side of the marked circle, placing the straight edge just outside the seamline and the other edge toward the center. Stitch the trim in place, overlapping ends to clean finish.

3 Pin and stitch the two circles together with right sides together and edges even, leaving a 6in opening.

4 Trim the seam and clip the curves. Turn right side out through the opening. Slipstitch the opening closed. Press the server flat.

5 Pin the doily to the center of the server. Sew the doily in place along the outside edge.

6 Fold the server in half and pin the edges together, taking care to match the segment markings. Stitch through all layers along marked lines, securing the threads with a knot at each end. Erase marked lines with water or just allow them to fade, depending on type of pen.

7 Tie the ribbon in a bow and sew it to center front of the doily.

To fit silver for a greater number of place settings, cut the circle a few inches larger, and divide the sections accordingly, choosing an even number.

To make this project simpler, apply the heart-shaped doilies with fabric glue, and use pinking shears to give an attractive zigzag edge which needs no hemming.

MOCK BALLOON VALANCE

Only one seam is required to make this pretty valance which imitates a raised balloon shade.

CHECKLIST

Materials

Decorator fabric
General sewing equipment
2½in-wide Continental curtain rod
Tissue paper

Techniques

Measuring up: windows	pp. 12–13
Installing window treatments	pp. 12–13
Joining fabric widths	pp. 14–15
Machine stitching	pp. 22–23

Measuring up

Measure the width of the window frame between its outside edges and the length down to the sill.

Cutting sizes

For the cutting length, divide the measured window length by 2; add 10½in.
For the cutting width, multiply the measured window width by 2½; add 4in.
Piece several widths of fabric together, if necessary, to achieve the total width. The valance will have a 2½:1 fullness ratio and will cover approximately one-quarter of the window length.
Cutting sizes include ½in seam allowance.

1 Turn under and press 2in on the short side edges of the panel. Tuck the cut edge in to meet the fold and press again. Topstitch the double hem along the inside fold.

2 Using an erasable pen, mark a stitching line 3½in from the top edge, on the right side of the fabric, and a fold line 5in from this edge.

3 Placing right sides together and cut edges even, stitch the long edges of the panel together forming a long tube. Allow a ½in seam. Press seam open. Turn valance right side out.

4 Pin valance layers together along previously marked fold line and press a crease. The seam and the marked stitching line are now on the back.

5 Pin layers together along seamline and stitching line. Stitch through all layers in the channel of the seam line and along marked stitching line to create the rod pocket.

6 To install the valance, slide it onto the rod distributing it evenly. Crumple several pieces of tissue paper and insert them into the valance to create the balloon fullness.

See page 63 for the finished article.

TENSION SHADE

The simplest of all shade assemblies was selected to show off some fabric too beautiful to pleat or gather.

CHECKLIST

Materials

Decorator fabric
Lining fabric
General sewing equipment
Liquid seam sealant
Paper-backed ⅜in-wide fusible web strip
Two tension rods

Techniques

Measuring up: windows	pp. 12–13
Joining fabric widths	pp. 14–15
Fusing fabric	pp. 24–25

Measuring up

Measure the width and length of the window inside the window frame. Determine the finished length: between one-quarter and one-half the measured length of the window.

Making the pattern

Decorator Fabric Panel For the cutting width, add 3in to the width of the window. For the cutting length, add 4in to the chosen finished length.
Lining Panel For the cutting width, add 1in to the measured width. For the cutting length, add 2in to the finished length.
Piece several widths of fabric together, if necessary, to achieve the total width. Depending upon the window size, the cutting width may exceed the cutting length. Cutting sizes include ½in seam allowance.

1 Using a liquid seam sealant, clean-finish the upper and lower edges of the decorator fabric.

2 Place the lining right side up. Apply a strip of fusible web to the seam allowance on both side edges.

3 Lay the decorator fabric right side up, and place the lining on top, right side down, with two side edges even and an equal amount of the decorator fabric showing at top and bottom. Fuse the lining to the decorator fabric along this edge.

4 Move the lining over so that its other side edge meets that of the decorator fabric. Fuse again.

5 Turn the shade right side out. Press the shade flat, allowing a 1in facing of fabric to wrap to the wrong side of the shade along each edge. Fuse the facing to the front of the shade along the short edges above and below the lining.

6 Apply a strip of fusible web to the wrong side of the decorator fabric along the top and bottom seam allowances.

7 Turn under 2in on the upper and lower edges of the shade and pin these edges in place. Press the creases and fuse these hems in place.

8 To install the shade, slide two tension rods through the top and bottom hems, and mount the rods inside the window molding, thus holding the shade taut between the two rods.

Pillowcase Café Curtains

Much of the sewing is completed before you begin when you use pillowcases for café-style curtains.

Measuring up

Measure the width and length of the window frame's outside edge down to the sill.

Cutting sizes

Valance The cutting width should be twice the measured window width. The length should be one-quarter the measured length plus 3in.
Curtains The cutting width of each curtain should equal the measured window width. The length should be one-half the measured window length plus 3in.
Cut open the pillowcases along the manufacturer's seams, and piece several together if necessary to achieve the total width and depth.
Cutting size includes ½in seam allowances.

1 Measuring from the hemmed edge of the pillowcase, mark the cutting length of the valance and curtains. Measure and mark the width of the valance and curtains, making sure to mark at a right angle to the hem.

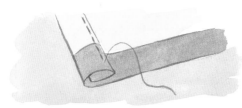

2 Turn under and press 2in on the side edges of each panel. Tuck the cut edge in to meet the fold and press again. Topstitch the hem in place along the inside fold.

3 Turn under and press ½in on the top edge of each panel. On the same edge, turn under 2½in and press again. Pin this heading in place along the first fold.

4 On all panels, stitch along the first, lower, fold. Measure and mark 1¼in up from the first line of stitching and stitch along the marked line.

5 Decide on the number of appliqués needed. Apply enough of the fusible web to the wrong side of the appliqué fabric to accommodate the size and number of appliqués. Do not remove the paper backing. Using the patterns provided, and placing them on the right side of the fabric, mark the shapes; cut them out. If you are using asymmetrical shapes, mark on the web side.

6 Position the appliqués on the hem of each piece; mark their positions lightly with a temporary marking pen. Remove the paper backing, and fuse the appliqué to the curtains and valance.

The decorative hem of the pillowcase provides the perfect background for simple fused appliqués. See pages 120–5 for templates. Instead of making your own appliqué motifs, you could see what is available readymade.

ARMCHAIR COVER

Fabric is simply draped over a club chair for an easy-to-sew slipcover.

CHECKLIST

Materials

Decorator fabric
Twisted decorator cord
½in-wide elastic or a drawstring
Metal eyelets to fit cord
General sewing equipment

Techniques

Joining fabric widths	pp. 14–15
Machine stitching	pp. 23–23
Hand stitching	pp. 22–23

Measuring up

Remove the seat cushion and measure its width, length, and thickness. Measure the width of the chair from the floor at the side, over the shoulder, across the back, and over the other shoulder down to the floor. Measure the length of the chair from the floor in front, across the seat, and over the back down to the floor.

Cutting sizes

Cushion The cutting width equals the length of the cushion plus twice the thickness plus 6in. The cutting length equals the length of the cushion plus twice the thickness plus 6in. *Chair* The cutting width is approximately ½yd greater than the measured width of the chair. Piece several fabric widths together, if necessary, to achieve cutting width. The cutting length is approximately ½yd greater than the measured length of the chair. Cutting sizes include ½in hem allowance.

1 Following the cutting dimensions, cut one cushion cover and one chair cover.

2 Use a dinner plate as a template to round off all the corners of each fabric piece.

To complete the cushion cover:

3 This step is optional, depending on the type of armchair. Turn under and press ¼in on all edges of the cushion cover. Turn under edges again, this time ¾in, and press. Pin, and stitch along the second fold, leaving a small opening to insert the elastic.

4 This step is also optional, depending on the type of armchair. Insert the elastic or a drawstring in the casing of the cushion cover. Place the cushion into the cover, draw the elastic tight and secure.

To complete the chair cover:

5 Turn under and press ½in on all edges of the chair cover. Turn up ½in again and press. Stitch close to the second fold.

6 Drape the cover over the chair, and arrange it so that the hem of the cover is even with the floor on all sides. Tuck the excess fabric into the gaps of the chair where the arms and back meet the deck of the seat to achieve this. If your cushion is removeable, follow step 4 and replace to secure the cover.

7 Measure the approximate depth from the bottom of the cushion to the floor. Collect the excess fabric at the four corners of the chair and hold the gathers together with a large safety pin at this measurement.

Here, the cover has been further simplified by using a decorative kilt pin to gather up the fabric at the corners.

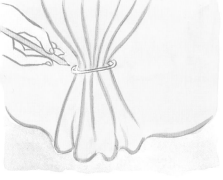

9 Cut a piece of decorative cord 1yd long for each corner of the chair. Slip the cord through the holes. Collect the excess fabric and tie a bow to secure. To prevent the cord ends from untwisting, tie a knot approximately 2in from each end of the cord, then fluff out the ends.

8 Mark the fabric where the gathering ends at each end of the safety pin. Remove the safety pin. Following the manufacturer's instructions, apply metal eyelets at the marks.

RUFFLED CHAIR CUSHION

A straight-backed wooden chair is made more comfortable with the addition of a foam block covered with fabric.

CHECKLIST

Materials

Decorator fabric
2in-thick polyurethane foam
1½yd grosgrain ribbon
General sewing equipment
Paper for pattern (optional)

Techniques

Machine stitching   pp. 22–23

Measuring up

Measure the width and length of the chair seat. If the seat is not a perfect rectangle, draw a paper pattern of the shape.

Cutting sizes

Foam block Add 2in to the width of the chair seat and 1in to the length; draw a rectangle to this size on the foam block. Or, if you have drawn a pattern of the seat, add 1in to the front and side edges of this pattern, then cut out this enlarged pattern and draw around it on the foam. Either cut the foam with an electric carving knife or have it professionally cut at a decorator's workroom.
Main piece Add 7in to the width of the foam block and 3½in to the depth. Or add 3½in to the front and side edges of the enlarged pattern used to cut the foam block.
Ruffle The cutting width is 5in. For the cutting length, measure the side and front edges of the foam block and multiply by 2½. Piece fabric widths together if necessary to achieve this length. Cutting sizes include ½in seam allowance.

1 Following the cutting dimensions, cut one each of the main piece and ruffle. Use a saucer as a template to round off the corners of the main piece.

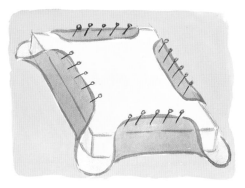

2 Lay the main piece on a flat surface, wrong side up, and place the foam block on top, centered. Fold the fabric edges over the foam and hold them in place with a few pins.

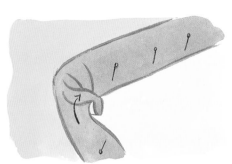

3 At each corner, form several small pleats in the fabric so that the fabric covers the foam neatly. Hand baste the pleats in place. Remove the foam block.

4 Turn under and press 1in on the short ends of the ruffle. Tuck the cut edges in to meet the folds and press again. Topstitch the double hems along the inner folds.

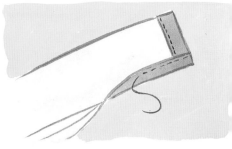

5 Hem one long edge of the ruffle, following the instructions in step 4.

6 Measure one side edge of the main cover piece, between the center of the two pleated areas. Make a note of this measurement. Similarly, measure the front edge and note its measurement. Multiply each measurement by 2½. On the cut edge of the ruffle, mark off the enlarged side and front edge measurements. (You may need to adjust the marks slightly in order to make the side sections of the ruffle even.)

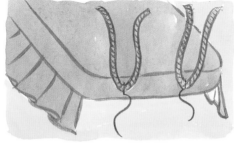

7 Placing right sides and cut edges together, pin the ruffle to one side edge of the main cover piece at two adjacent corners. Fold the fabric into seven or eight even pleats, and pin these in place. Repeat on the front edge and the other side edge.

8 Hand baste the ruffle to the main cover, then stitch them together, press the seam flat and clean-finish the seam allowances. Insert the foam block in the cover.

9 Cut the grosgrain ribbon in half. Find the center point of each piece, and sew this to the back edge of the cushion cover just behind the side struts of the chair, taking care not to sew into the foam. Tie the ribbons around the chair struts to hold the cushion in place. Trim the ribbon ends neatly.

The pleats of this ruffle give a neat effect on this easy-to-make cushion cover. For a softer look you could simply gather the ruffle.

SLIPCOVERED SOFA

A large rectangle is thrown over a large sofa and held in place with decorator cord or fringe.

1 Following the cutting dimensions, cut one rectangle of fabric. Use a dinner plate as a template to round off the corners of the cover.

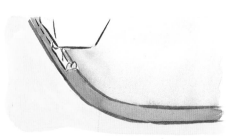

2 Turn under and press ½in on all edges. Turn under another ½in and press. Stitch close to the second fold.

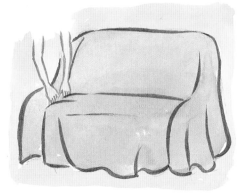

3 Drape the cover over the sofa. Tuck the excess fabric into the gaps where the arms and back meet the seat cushions, until the hem of the cover is even with the floor on all sides. Alternatively, tuck some fabric into the gaps and allow the excess to puddle on the floor on all sides of the sofa.

4 Measure the approximate depth from the bottom of the cushions to the floor. Collect the excess fabric at the four corners of the sofa and hold the gathers together with a large safety pin at this level.

5 Wrap a length of heavy twisted decorator cord or very wide bullion fringe around the base of the sofa. Join the ends of the trimming together at the back with safety pins. Secure it to the fabric at random points with more safety pins, hidden from view.

The hem of the cover is made even with the floor by tucking the excess fabric into the gaps of the sofa where the arms and back meet the seat cushion. Use fusible web to hem the fabric for a no-sew alternative.

SPLENDID SEATS

As a clever alternative to time-consuming tailored slip covers, cover your sofa or chairs with wrap and tie casual slip covers. To protect the upholstery underneath, choose durable fabric and a dark color – perfect for families with young children. To make a holiday party more festive, make something new for your sofa to wear. Or for a welcome change of pace, choose a pastel print for the warm summer months and a cozy plaid for the winter. These covers are so simple and appealing, you will want to make several.

Tied seat cover
Bring your old chair to life with an easy-to-make tied seat cover. Cut enough material so that it hangs over the edge, remove excess material at the corners and attach ribbon or decorator cord to hold the cover in place. This is so quick and easy that it can be used as a permanent cover or to temporarily change the appearance of a room for a special occasion.

Covered pouffe
Give an old pouffe a facelift with a generous draping of fabric and attractively knotted cords.

Ruffled arm chair cover

A rich, dramatic color was chosen for this ruched chair cover. A long strip of the fabric was used to cover the chair from the bottom front, over the cushion and the top and down the back. For a temporary cover, secure it with safety pins or stitch in place for a long-term furnishing change. The arms are made from separate pieces of material. At the top of the arm, sew a couple of rows of long, irregular running stitches. Pull on the threads to gather the ruches and tie off. Tuck one side of the fabric beneath the cushion and allow the rest to puddle on the floor.

Stool

Try this no sew, no fuss method of covering a child's stool. Glue foam to the stool top, then place quilt batting and fabric on top. Turn stool upside down and ensure that it is centered on the fabric. Gently pull fabric taut and, using a staple gun, attach to the underneath of the stool.

BALLOON SHADE

A slightly more ambitious
project, this balloon shade
is reminiscent of the
Victorian era.

Measuring up

Measure the window frame between its
outside edges and from the mounting board
position to the sill.

Cutting sizes

Shade For the cutting width multiply the
measured width of the window by 2. For the
cutting length, multiply the measured length
of the window by 1⅓.
Piece several widths of fabric together, if
necessary, to achieve the total width.
The shade will have a 2 : 1 fullness ratio.
Rod cover The cutting length is the length of
the meter rod plus 1½in. The width is the
circumference of the rod plus 1¼in.

1 Turn under and press 2in on
each side edge. Tuck the edge in to
meet the fold and press again. Open
out the second fold. Apply fusible
web to the hem along the folded
edge. Remove the paper backing,
refold the hem, and fuse in place.

2 Measuring from the folded edges,
divide the shade width into equal
thirds and mark these divisions on
the wrong side. The distance between
the marks should be not less than
12in. For wide windows, mark out
more divisions and fewer for smaller
windows.

3 Trim one end of the ring tape, so
that the first ring is 1½in from the cut
edge. Measuring from this cut,
leading edge, cut a length of ring tape
equal to the cutting length of the
shade.

Note: If the rings are too close to the
edge to press the hem, carefully
remove the stitches from these rings
and discard them.

4 Cut three more pieces of ring
tape, identical to the first.

5 Position each ring tape on the
wrong side of the shade, along the
side hems and marked lines, with the
leading edge at the bottom. Pin the
tape to the shade with the first ring
positioned 2½in from the lower edge
of the shade.

6 Pin each tape to the shade,
keeping the tapes parallel and the
rings directly opposite each other.
Trim the tapes 1in below the upper
edge of the shade. Carefully fuse the
ring tape to the side hems and
marked lines.

7 Turn under and press 1in on
the upper edge. Following the
manufacturer's instructions, apply
fusible web to the hem along the
folded edge. Remove the paper
backing, refold the hem, and fuse in
place, covering the cut edge of the
ring tape.

Easy-to-use fusible shirring tape and ring tape create both the crosswise and lengthwise fullness and simplify the construction of this lavish balloon shade.

8 Cut a length of shirring tape equal to the width of the shade. Apply the tape to the upper edge of the shade between the side hems.

9 Turn under and press 2in on the lower edge. Tuck the edge in to meet the fold, and press again.

10 Open out the second fold. Following the manufacturer's instructions, apply fusible web to this hem.

11 Stitch or fuse one or two rows of tassel fringe to the lower edge of the shade, turning under the ends to clean-finish.

12 Fold the rod cover in half lengthwise, with right sides facing. Stitch the long edges together and across one end. Trim seam allowances, and, with the help of a knitting needle, turn right side out.

13 Slip the cover over the metal rod. Trim the end if necessary, turn it under, and sew it closed. Sew the rod in place at the lower edge of the shade, just under each ring, with a few hand stitches through the fabric.

14 Cut a length of cord for each ring tape, each measuring twice the length of the shade plus the width. Tie each cord securely to a bottom ring and thread it up through all the other rings.

15 Attach a screw eye to the mounting board at the position of each ring tape. Draw up the shirring tape at the top of the shade, and adjust the gathers evenly. Mount the shade on the board. Thread each cord through a screw eye and take all to one side of the window. With the shade down, tie the cords in a knot. Trim ends as necessary.

FRINGED DRAPERY

For a striking drapery, trim a single panel of fabric with heavy bullion fringe and hang it from a decorative rod.

C H E C K L I S T

Materials

Heavyweight decorator fabric
6in bullion fringe
⅜in-wide ribbon
General sewing equipment
Fabric glue

Techniques

Measuring up: windows	pp. 12–13
Installing window treatments	pp. 12–13
Joining fabric widths	pp. 14–15
Machine stitching	pp. 22–23
Hand stitching	pp. 22–23

Measuring up

Measure the width of the window frame between its outside edges. Measure the length from the rod to the floor.

Cutting sizes

Drapery Panel For the cutting width, multiply the window width by 2. For the cutting length, subtract the width of the fringe from the window length, then add 3in.
Tieback Cut one rectangle 9 x 29in.
Piece several widths of fabric together if necessary to achieve the total drapery width. The drapery will have a 2:1 fullness ratio, and the lower edge of the fringe will hang ½in above the floor. If you wish the drapery to puddle on the floor, add 15in. The cutting measurements allow for a 1½in-deep rod pocket. Increase the cutting length for a thicker rod.
Cutting sizes include ½in seam allowance.

1 Turn under and press 1in on the lower edge. Tuck the cut edge in to meet the fold and press again. Stitch along the second fold.

2 Turn under and press 1in on each side edge. Tuck the cut edge in to meet the fold and press again. Stitch along the second fold.

3 On the right side of the fabric, stitch or glue the header of the fringe to the hems of the drape, so that the fringe itself extends past the drapery hem. Begin and end at the cut upper edge of the drape, and miter the corners at the lower edge.

4 Turn under and press ½in on the upper edge of the drape. Turn under and press a further 1½in. Insert the decorative rod in the rod pocket to double check this measurement. Adjust the width, if necessary, and remove the rod. Stitch along the first fold.

To make the tieback:

5 Fold the rectangle in half lengthwise with right sides facing. Stitch together both short ends and the one long edge, leaving a small opening for turning.

6 Turn the fabric right side out, and slipstitch the opening edges together. Press the tieback flat.

7 On one side, sew or glue the header of the fringe to the lower and side edges of the tieback. Begin and end at the upper edge of the drape, turning under the end of the fringe. Miter the corners at the lower edge.

8 Cut two 3in pieces of ribbon. Make each into a small loop and sew to the upper corners of the tieback.

Gluing the decorative fringe in place eliminates the task of sewing through a heavy trimming.

FUSED AND PLEATED DRAPERIES

Making this classic drapery style is simplified by the use of fused hems and pleater tape.

CHECKLIST

Materials

Decorator fabric
Paper-backed ⅜in-wide fusible web strip
Fusible pleater tape
General sewing equipment

Techniques

Measuring up: windows	pp. 12–13
Installing window treatments	pp. 12–13
Joining fabric widths	pp. 14–15
Machine stitching	pp. 22–23
Fusing fabric	pp. 24–25

Measuring up

Measure the length of the window from the rod to the floor.

Cutting sizes

Because calculating the cutting size of the draperies is a rather lengthy procedure, this information is given in the main project instructions, steps 1–5.
Cutting sizes include ½in seam allowance.

1 ▷ The pleated width of the drapery will equal the measured length of the mounted rod plus two returns to the wall. For each drapery, divide this calculated distance by 2 and add the center overlap – about 2in.

2 ▷ The cutting dimensions will be determined by the window width and the spacing between pockets on the type of pleater tape purchased. The cutting width of each drapery will measure approximately three times the finished width. For an exact measurement, first insert pleater hooks in the drapery tape, leaving the desired spacing between pleats.

3 ▷ Hook the pleater tape to the rod with the first pleat positioned at the outside corner. Allow the tape to lie flat in the return area from the front corner of the rod to the wall and in the center overlap area between the two panels. Mark the pleater tape at the wall and the front end.

4 ▷ Measure the finished length of the draperies from the top of the pleater tape to the floor, and record this measurement.

5 ▷ Remove the tape from the rod and the hooks from the tape. To the marks made, add ½in to each end for the cutting length of the pleater tape.

The cutting width of each panel is equal to the finished length of the pleater tape, plus 8in for side hems. For the cutting length of each panel, take the measured length and add twice the width of the pleater tape plus 8in for the lower hem.

Piece two or more widths of fabric together, if necessary, to achieve the total drapery width. The drapery panels should be exactly the same size.

6▶ Following the cutting dimensions, cut two panels.

To make one panel:

7▶ Turn under and press 8in on the lower edge. Tuck the cut edge in to meet the fold and press again.

8▶ Open out the second fold. Following the manufacturer's instructions, apply fusible web to the hem along the folded edge. Remove the paper backing, refold the hem, and fuse in place.

9▶ To hem the side edges of the drapery, repeat steps 7 and 8 making an initial fold of 4in, instead of 8in.

10▶ On the upper edge, turn under twice the width of the pleater tape; press. Tuck the cut edge in to meet the fold and press again.

11▶ Open out the second fold. Following the manufacturer's instructions, apply fusible web to the hem along the folded edge. Remove the paper backing, refold the hem, and fuse in place.

12▶ Pin the pleater tape to the center of the upper hem. Turn under the ends to clean-finish, and stitch through all layers on all edges of the tape.

13▶ Leaving the returns flat, insert the hooks in the tape. Hang the draperies from the rod.

These draperies look difficult to make, but the relatively simple measuring method and the use of pleater tape put them within anyone's capabilities.

SPIRALING TASSELS

A center swag and spiraling tails make an unusual window treatment.

CHECKLIST

Materials

Decorator fabric
Tassel braid
Fusible shirring tape
Hook and loop tape
General sewing equipment
Mounting board and hardware

Techniques

Measuring windows	pp. 12–13
Installing window treatments	pp. 12–13
Fusing fabric	pp. 24–25
Machine stitching	pp. 22–23

Measuring up

Measure the width of the window frame between the outside edges and the length to the floor. Use a cord to determine the length of the swag. Fasten one end to the wall or window frame at the chosen position for the lower edge after gathering, then drape the cord down and up to the corresponding point on the other side. Measure the cord.

Cutting sizes

Swag The cutting width is 18in. The cutting length is equal to the measured swag length plus 1in.
Tails The cutting width is 18in. For the cutting length, double the measured window length. Cutting sizes include ½in hem allowance.

1 Following the cutting dimensions, cut one swag and two tails. Add 1in to the measured window width; record this measurement and mark it off in the center of one long edge of the swag rectangle. Draw a straight line from the marks to the adjacent corners, and trim the ends to create the swag shape.

2 Clean-finish all the cut edges on all the pieces.

3 Turn under and press ½in on all the edges of all the pieces. Stitch ⅜in from folded edge.

4 Following the manufacturer's instructions, apply the shirring tape to each angled side edge of the swag on the wrong side of the fabric. Do not pull the cords yet.

5 Apply the shirring tape to the other long edge of each tail on the wrong side of the fabric. Pull the shirring tape cords to gather the fabric.

6 Stitch the tassel braid to the inner long edge of each tail (the edge that will hang nearer the center) and to the lower edge, on the right side of the fabric.

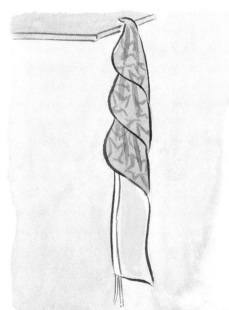

7 Because shirring tapes gather at different rates, check the length of the tail by temporarily attaching it to the mounting board. Pull the shirring tape cords and allow the tail to spiral toward the floor. Adjust the gathers until the shirred edge is hidden by the hemmed edge on each spiral.

Trim the fabric to adjust the length if necessary. Remove the fabric from the board. Secure the cords by knotting at both ends.

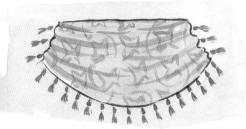

8 On the right side of the fabric, stitch the tassel braid to the two short edges and lower long edge of the swag. Pull the shirring tape cords to gather the fabric. Secure the cord ends by knotting them.

9 Cut the hook and loop tape to equal the window width. Stitch the loop (fuzzy) half of the tape to the wrong side of the swag, on the untrimmed edge.

10 Staple or glue the hook (stiff) half of the tape to the top of the mounting board at the edge closest to the wall.

11 Staple the top edge of each tail to the top of the mounting board at the side. Position the swag over the tails on the installed mounting board by joining the hook and loop tapes.

The swag and tails can be used with matching floor-length draperies, as shown, or hung by themselves over shutters or a Venetian blind.

To make the no-sew version of this, use a liquid seam sealant to clean-finish the edges, fusible web tape for the hems, and fabric glue to apply the tassel braid.

ZIGZAG VALANCE

A rod pocket is not needed for this valance, since the weight of the fabric holds it in place.

CHECKLIST

Materials

Decorator fabric
Braid trim and tassels
General sewing equipment
Paper for pattern

Techniques

Making patterns	pp. 16–17
Machine stitching	pp. 22–23

Measuring up

Measure the length of the mounted rod. Measure the length of the window from the rod to the sill. The valance will be two-thirds this length, so that, when hung, it will cover one-third of the window.

Cutting sizes

Valance and *Lining* For the cutting width, add 1in to the measured length of the rod. For the cutting length, add 1in to the finished length.
Piece several fabric widths together, if necessary, to achieve the cutting widths. Cutting sizes include ⅛in seam allowance.

1 For best results, make a paper pattern, following the instructions given in steps 2–7, and mount the pattern on the rod to check its proportions before cutting the decorator fabrics.

2 Following the cutting dimensions, cut the basic rectangle.

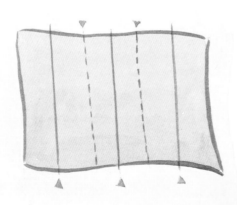

3 For the distance between points, divide the finished width of the valance by 3. For very wide windows, divide by a greater number. Mark this distance the appropriate number of times at the top edge of the pattern. Mark the same distance along the bottom edge, but split the measurement at the two sides.

4 Find the horizontal center of the valance. Mark two lines across the center of the valance 6in apart.

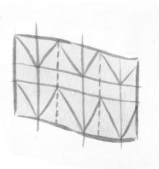

5 On the lower of these lines, mark the previously determined distance between points. On the upper line, mark the distance, but split the measurement at the two sides.

6 Matching the marks, draw three whole points at the lower edge and two whole and two half points at the upper edge.

7 Cut the pattern along the diagonal lines, trimming away the upper and lower triangles.

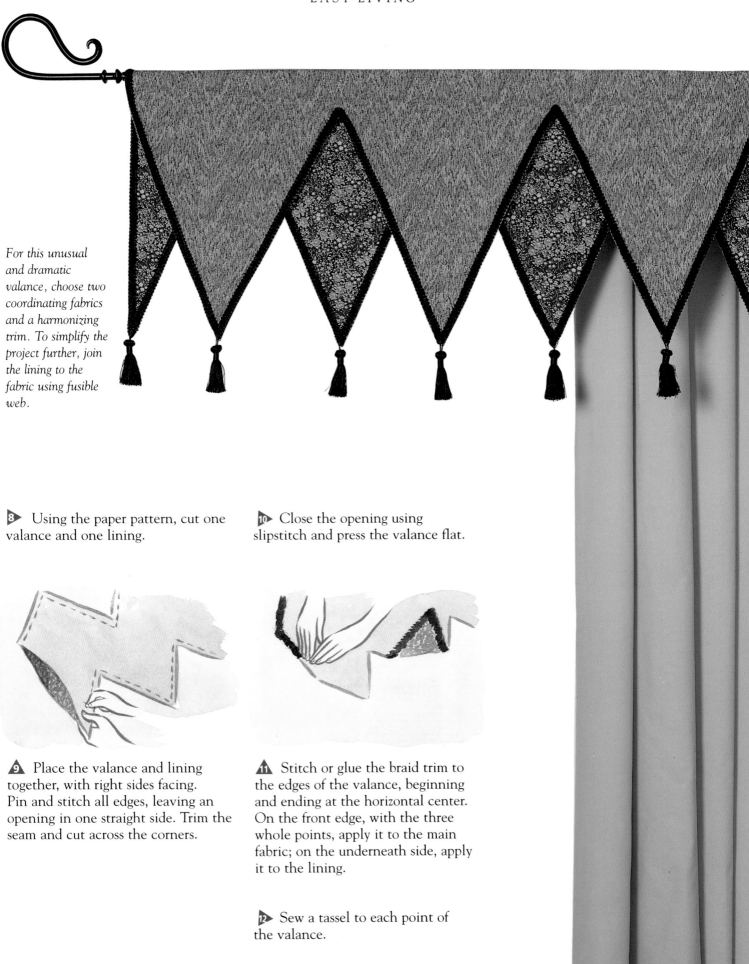

For this unusual
and dramatic
valance, choose two
coordinating fabrics
and a harmonizing
trim. To simplify the
project further, join
the lining to the
fabric using fusible
web.

8▶ Using the paper pattern, cut one valance and one lining.

10▶ Close the opening using slipstitch and press the valance flat.

9▶ Place the valance and lining together, with right sides facing. Pin and stitch all edges, leaving an opening in one straight side. Trim the seam and cut across the corners.

11▶ Stitch or glue the braid trim to the edges of the valance, beginning and ending at the horizontal center. On the front edge, with the three whole points, apply it to the main fabric; on the underneath side, apply it to the lining.

12▶ Sew a tassel to each point of the valance.

ROD POCKET VALANCE

This easy-to-make valance slips over an extra-wide curtain rod attached to a fabric-covered cornice board.

C H E C K L I S T

Materials

Printed decorator fabric
Solid decorator fabric
General sewing equipment
4½in-wide Continental curtain rod

Techniques

Measuring up: windows	pp. 12–13
Installing window treatments	pp. 12–13
Joining fabric widths	pp. 14–15
Machine stitching	pp. 22–23

Measuring up

Measure the window frame between its outside edges.

Making the pattern

Rod Sleeve and Headings The cutting width is 6in. For the cutting length, multiply the measured window width by 3.
Back Facing The cutting width is 16in. For the cutting length, multiply the measured window width by 3.
Piece several widths of fabric together if necessary, to achieve cutting lengths.
Cutting sizes include ½in seam allowance.

1 Following the cutting dimensions, cut one rod sleeve from solid fabric. Cut two headings and one facing from printed fabric.

2 On one heading, measure 3in up from one long edge on a short edge; mark this point. Fold the heading in half crosswise, and mark the other long edge 3in in from the fold. Draw a tapered line between the marks. Cut along the line through both layers. Save one trimmed-off piece for use later.

3 Open the folded heading. Using the trimmed heading as a pattern, cut the other heading the same shape. If you are using a directional fabric, the shaping should be applied to the lower edge on the second heading.

4 Using the trimmed-off piece from step 2 as a pattern, shape the upper and lower edges of the facing.

5 Placing right sides and long straight edges together, stitch the headings to the rod pocket. Press the seams open.

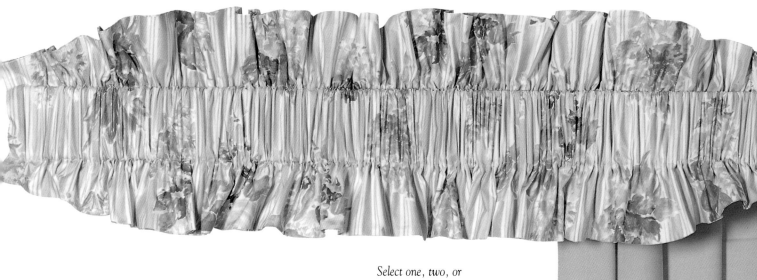

Select one, two, or three coordinating fabrics for this easy-to-sew rod cover.

As an alternative to hemming the ends with stitching use strips of fusible web.

6 Turn under and press 2in on one short end of the header-sleeve assembly. Tuck the cut edge in to meet the fold and press again. Topstitch the double hem along the inside fold. Repeat for the opposite short end.

7 Repeat step 6 on the facing.

8 With right sides facing, stitch the front assembly to the facing along the upper and lower edges. Trim the seam allowances, clip the curves, and press the seams open.

9 Turn the valance right side out and press flat. Pin the layers together along the rod pocket and heading seams. Stitch through all the layers in the ditch of the seams, backstitching and tying threads securely at the ends.

WINNING WINDOWS

Whether you wish to make a grand statement with one graceful sweep of fabric or just add a little color with a small ruffled valance, choose from one of the many sewing and fusing techniques provided to make an interesting window treatment. Follow easy measuring techniques for making simple rectangles and circles to create clever curtains and shades for any size window. Frame the view, control the light and increase your privacy with a few carefully placed seams and hems.

Draped swag *Disguised as an intricate custom-made swag, this simple-to-make draped swag is created using long* rectangles of fabric and lace. Fold the fabrics into wide accordion-style pleats before draping it over a decorative brass pole. For very long swags, pin the folds together with extra large safety pins until it is on the pole and ready to be arranged.

Roman shade *Attractive and easy-to-make, the Roman shade could be the perfect choice for many of the rooms* in your home. By using fusible web for the hemming and fusible ring tape for the gathering, this sophisticated window treatment becomes both simple and satisfying to complete.

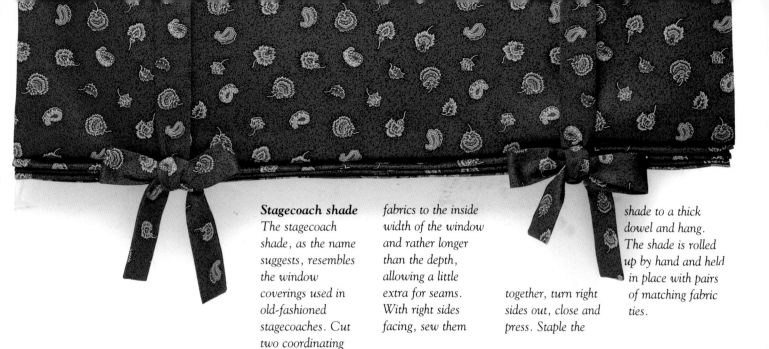

Stagecoach shade

The stagecoach shade, as the name suggests, resembles the window coverings used in old-fashioned stagecoaches. Cut two coordinating fabrics to the inside width of the window and rather longer than the depth, allowing a little extra for seams. With right sides facing, sew them together, turn right sides out, close and press. Staple the shade to a thick dowel and hang. The shade is rolled up by hand and held in place with pairs of matching fabric ties.

Dish towel cafe curtains

Dish towels used as the fabric for a simple window treatment make a truly coordinated kitchen. Follow the instructions for making the Pillowcase cafe curtains on page 42. You could create an attractive fringed edge to your curtains by cutting off the hem and unpicking a little of the fabric. Depending on the size of your curtains, it may be better to use a different loosely-woven fabric rather than dish towels.

Mock balloon valance

For instructions on how to make this original window treatment, see page 40.

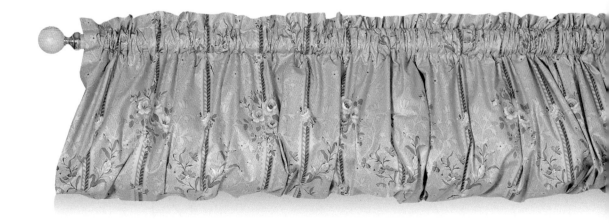

FABRIC SCREEN

Refurbish an old screen or decorate a new one with some fabric and painted floral motifs.

C H E C K L I S T

Materials

Wooden room divider screen
Decorator fabric
⅜in-wide fusible web strip
General sewing equipment
Acrylic paint and brushes
Varnish

Techniques

Machine stitching	pp. 22–23
Fusing fabric	pp. 24–25

Measuring up

Measure the width of the screen opening. Measure the length of the opening from the front of the screen, over the upper dowel, around the lower dowel and up to the front again.

Cutting sizes

For the cutting width of the fabric, multiply the measured width of the opening by 2. For the cutting length of the fabric, take the total measured length and add twice the depth of the gathered heading plus 1in. The fabric will have a 2:1 fullness ratio.
Multiply cutting sizes by the number of panels in the screen.
Cutting sizes include ½in seam allowance and 1in hems.

1 If you are using a new screen, assemble it up to the point of attaching the hinges. Prepare the wood and apply a base coat of paint to the screen. Allow to dry, and if necessary apply a second coat. If you are using an old screen, remove the hardware and hinges.

2 Transfer your design to the top of the screen (see also *Template section* at the end of the book). You may need to enlarge or reduce the size of the flowers using a photocopier. By cutting apart sections of the design, you can alter the length or change the shape of the curve.

3 Using contrasting colors, paint the details of the design. Allow to dry thoroughly. Apply varnish and complete the screen assembly.

To make one fabric panel:

4 Following the manufacturer's instructions, apply fusible web to the wrong side of the fabric on each long side edge of each fabric panel.

5 Turn under 1in on both long side edges of the fabric panel; fuse the hems in place.

The transfer pattern can be altered in size and shape to fit almost any screen.

6 Pin and stitch the short ends of the panel together to create a loop of fabric. Press the seam open and turn the panel right side out.

8 Remove the dowel rods from the screen and slip the fabric panel over them. Distribute the fullness evenly.

7 Measure off to one side of the seam a distance twice the desired depth of the heading. Position the seam over this point. Stitch in the ditch of the seamline through both layers, backstitching at the ends to secure.

Sew-Free Lampshades

Fusible shirring tape applied to one or both edges creates the gathers on these clever covers.

C H E C K L I S T

Materials

Conical lampshade
Decorator or eyelet fabric
Fusible shirring tape
Fusible web strip
Ribbon or trimming
Fabric glue

Techniques

Fusing fabric   pp. 24–25

Measuring up

Measure the circumference of the lampshade at the narrower upper edge only. Measure the height of the lampshade from edge to edge. Note: This cover is not suitable for conical shades on which the circumference of the lower edge is more than 3 times that of the upper edge.

Cutting sizes

Shirred Lampshade For the cutting width, add 1in to the height of the shade.
Hemmed Lampshade For the cutting width, add 3in to the height of the shade.
Eyelet Lampshade For the cutting width, add ½in to the height of the shade. Measure and cut the fabric to include the scalloped edge.
All lampshades For the cutting length, multiply the measured circumference by 3.

1 ▶ Turn under and press ½in on the long upper edge of the lampshade cover.

2 ▶ Treat the lower edge of the cover in the following manner for each style of shade:

• For the Shirred Lampshade, turn under and press ½in.

• For the Hemmed Lampshade, turn under and press 2in. Tuck the cut edge in to meet the fold and press again. Apply fusible web to the inside of the hem, and fuse in place.

• For the Eyelet Lampshade, no finishing is required at the lower edge.

3 ▲ On one short edge of the cover turn under and press ½in. Apply a strip of fusible web to the seam allowance.

4 ▲ Place the cut short edges together, and fuse the seam, creating a cylindrical shape.

5 ▶ For the Shirred Lampshade, cut two lengths of shirring tape equal to the distance around the cover.
• For the Hemmed and the Eyelet Lampshades, cut one length of shirring tape equal to the circumference of the cover. Beginning and ending at the seam, apply the tape either to the top edge, or to both edges of the cover on the wrong side, ¼in from the fold.

6 Pull the cords of the tape to fit one or both edges of the lampshade, depending on the style, distributing the gathers evenly. Secure the cords with a knot, and trim excess cord. Glue the cover to the shade at one or both edges.

Note: For easy removal of the cover, use very little glue, applying it in small dabs at the upper edge only.

7 Glue a bow or some braid trim to the top edge of the cover.

These no-sew lampshade covers allow you to transform a lamp either permanently or just temporarily – for a summery look, perhaps.

NO-SEW PILLOWS

No sewing is required to make these pillows. Each can be made from readymade items found in a home decorating department.

C H E C K L I S T

Materials

Square and neck roll pillow form
Scarves, napkins, pillowcases, and/or fabric
Ribbon or trimming
Safety pins or rubber bands
General sewing equipment
Fabric glue

Measuring up

Measure the width and length of the square pillow form. Measure the length of the neck roll form.

1 Purchase one pillowcase with a decorative hem and a neck roll pillow form. You will also need 4 rubber bands, 2 yards of ribbon, and 5 ribbon roses.

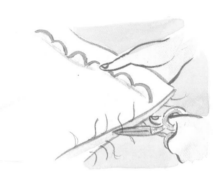

2 Cut open the pillowcase along the long and short seams. Do not un-stitch the hem. Press flat.

3 Turn under the long edges of the case, which run perpendicular to the hem, so that the distance between the folds is 10in greater than the length of the neck roll form. Press the folds.

4 Beginning at the cut end, opposite the hem, roll the pillowcase around the form. Gather up the pillowcase at both ends of the form and wrap with rubber bands. Tie a ribbon around both ends, finishing with a bow. Glue ribbon roses along the hemline.

For the Lace Scarf Pillow

1 Purchase one lace dresser scarf no wider than the chosen square pillow form and 2–3 times its size in length. Cut a square of fabric 2½ times the size of the form. You will also need 6 small safety pins and 1 yd of ribbon.

2 Place the fabric wrong side up and lay the form in the center. In the same way as you would cover a gift box, fold opposite ends of the fabric around the form and pin in place.

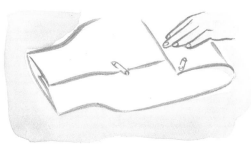

3 Now fold the opposite ends of the fabric around the form and pin in place. On the last fold, hide the pins under the fabric.

4 Place the covered form on the center of the lace scarf. Wrap the scarf ends to the right side of the form and fold back any excess. Thread the ends of the ribbon through the lace holes on both sides of the scarf. Tie the ribbon into a bow.

To make this Pillowcase Neck Roll, a pillowcase wrapped around a neck roll form is trimmed with ribbon roses and satin ribbons.

The attractive Lace Scarf Pillow is made using fabric and a lace dresser scarf. They cover a square pillow form and are secured with safety pins and a bow.

LOW-SEW PILLOWS

Very few seams were needed to make these simple pillows. Decorator's twisted cord and buttons add the finishing touch.

CHECKLIST

Materials

Square and rectangular pillow form
Decorator fabrics
Buttons and cord
General sewing equipment

Techniques

Machine stitching   pp. 22–23

Measuring up

Measure the width and length of the pillow.

Cutting sizes

Tied Bag Pillow
For the cutting width, multiply the width/length of the square pillow form by 2 and add 1in. For the length, multiply by 2½.
Button Pillow
Center For the cutting width, add 1in to the width of the pillow form. For the cutting length, multiply the length of the form by 2 and add 1in.
Borders The cutting width is 7in. For the cutting length, multiply the length of the form by 2 and add 1in.
Cutting sizes include ½in seam allowance.

To make the Tied Bag Pillow:

1 Following the cutting dimensions, cut one cover from decorator fabric.

2 Fold the cover in half lengthwise with right sides facing. Pin and stitch the long side edge and the lower end of the cover. Clean-finish the seams and press them open.

3 Measuring from the lower seam, mark the size of the pillow form on the seamed and folded edges. Fold down the cut edge at the open end to meet these marks. Press the fold.

4 Turn the cover right side out. Insert the form and tie the opening closed with decorative cord, wrapping the cord several times around the opening.

To make the Button Pillow:

1 Following the cutting dimensions, cut one center from decorator fabric and two borders from a coordinating fabric.

2 Fold the borders in half lengthwise with wrong sides together; press. Place the center piece right side up, and pin the borders to its long edges with all raw edges matching; stitch. Clean-finish the seams and press toward the center.

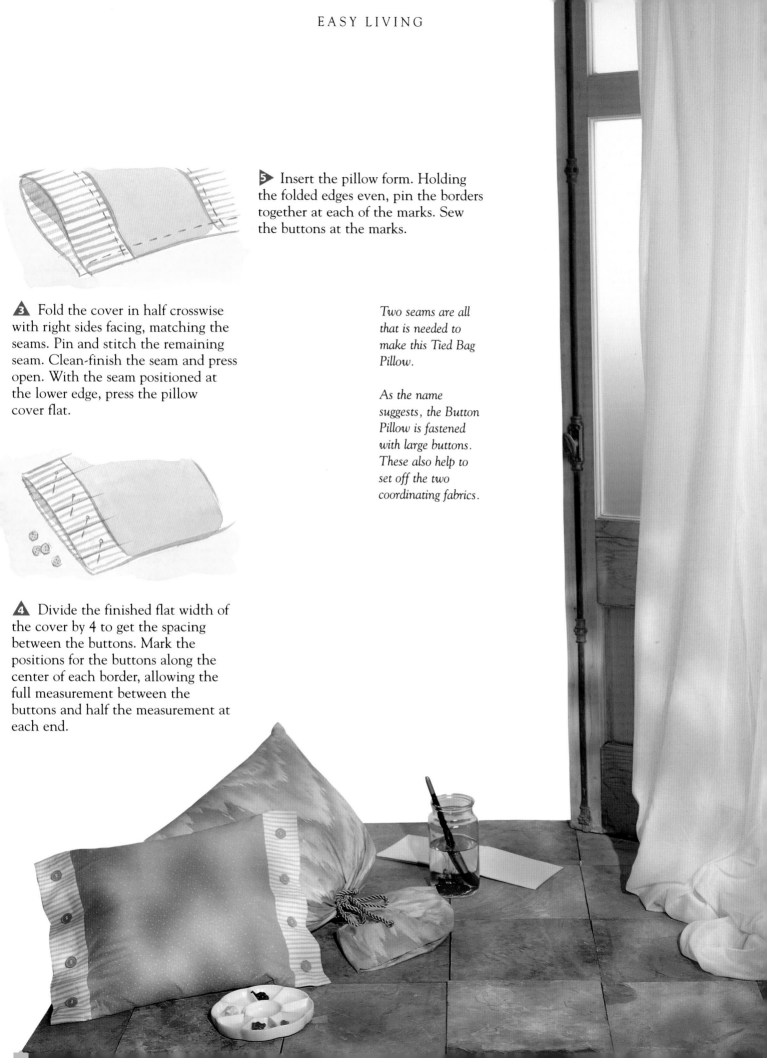

5 Insert the pillow form. Holding the folded edges even, pin the borders together at each of the marks. Sew the buttons at the marks.

3 Fold the cover in half crosswise with right sides facing, matching the seams. Pin and stitch the remaining seam. Clean-finish the seam and press open. With the seam positioned at the lower edge, press the pillow cover flat.

Two seams are all that is needed to make this Tied Bag Pillow.

As the name suggests, the Button Pillow is fastened with large buttons. These also help to set off the two coordinating fabrics.

4 Divide the finished flat width of the cover by 4 to get the spacing between the buttons. Mark the positions for the buttons along the center of each border, allowing the full measurement between the buttons and half the measurement at each end.

PILLOW TALK

Add sparkle and interest to any room with easy-to-make throw pillows. Carefully chosen colors and textures help to carry the eye around the room and unify the space creating the look of a professionally decorated room. Coordinate the entire room by using decorator fabric left over from the window treatment or choose a contrasting fabric to introduce an additional color. Pillows and accessories require little yardage making them a perfect choice for luxurious and elegant fabrics which may be too costly to use for larger projects. For an interesting change of pace, try the pillow projects which substitute bed sheets and table linens for decorator fabric.

Scarf pillow
This simple no-sew pillow was made using two attractive floral scarves held together on each side of the pillow form with coordinating decorator cord.

Fringed napkin pillow
Take two plaid napkins that are slightly larger than the pillow form and tie them together at the corners.

Cracker-style pillow
This attractive pillow is simple to produce. Hem your fabric with fusible web, then roll it around the bolster and secure the ends using coordinating ribbon.

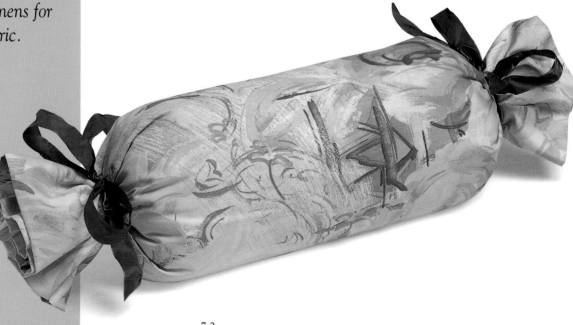

Try a more dramatic
style using
contrasting colored
fabrics, as pictured
here. The impact is
increased by using
generous amounts of
luxurious fabric.

DESK ACCESSORIES

This handy desk blotter and file folder will give a touch of class to your desk or work station.

C H E C K L I S T

Materials

Decorator fabric
Multi-pocket file folder
2yd 1in-wide ribbon
Artist's and poster board
Lightweight quilt batting
Paper-backed fusible web and fabric glue
Paper blotter

Techniques

Cutting shapes	pp. 16–17
Fusing fabric	pp. 24–25

Measuring up

Measure the paper blotter and the file holder (front and back) in both directions.

Cutting sizes

Desk Blotter
Base Board Cut the board equal in width and 4in longer than the paper blotter.
Base Fabric and Fusible Web Cut 4in wider and longer than the base board.
Side Boards, Batting Cut the length equal to the width of base board; cutting width is 4in.
Side Fabric Cut 4in wider and longer than the side boards.
File Folder
Board Front and Back Cut to the same size as the front and back of the file folder.
Quilt Batting Cut the quilt batting the same size as the back of the file folder.
Fabric Front and Back Cut each front and back piece 4in wider and longer than the boards.

1 Following the cutting dimensions, use the mat knife to cut two base boards and side boards from artist's board. Cut one base from fusible web and two side pieces from quilt batting.

2 Following the manufacturer's instructions, apply the fusible web to the wrong side of the base fabric.

3 Place one base board on the ironing board. Remove the paper backing from the fabric and center the fabric, right side up, on the board. Fuse it in place, taking care not to iron over the edges.

4 Turn the board wrong side up. Wrap each corner over board, and fuse it in place.

5 Wrap the straight edges of the fabric to the back of the board, and fuse in place.

6 Glue the quilt batting to one side of each side board.

7 Lay a side fabric piece wrong side up, and position a side board, batting side down, in the center of the fabric. Wrap one long straight edge of the fabric over the edge of the board, and glue it in place. Repeat on the other side board.

8 On the remaining long edge and two short edges of the board, about 1in in, apply fabric glue. Place the board on one side edge of the base board with the fabric-covered edge toward the center and the other edges aligned. Allow the glue to dry. Repeat with the other side board.

9▶ Turn the board wrong side up. Wrap each corner of the fabric to the back of the board, and glue it in place. Then glue the straight edges in place.

10▶ Take the remaining base board and glue it to the back of the base board, hiding all cut edges of the fabrics. Place weights, such as heavy books, over the blotter overnight to help the glued layers to bond. Insert the paper blotter.

To cover the file folder:

11▶ Following the cutting dimensions, cut one front and one back from poster board. Cut one front fabric piece following the straight grain and a back piece following the bias grain. Cut a back piece from quilt batting.

12▶ Glue the quilt batting to one side of the back board.

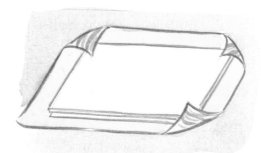

13▶ Wrap the boards in the fabric and glue to the wrong side, beginning with the corners, then gluing the straight edges.

14▶ Glue the center of the ribbon to the back of the file folder. Glue the front board to the front of the file folder and the back board to the back, over the ribbon. Place the file under weights to dry overnight. Tie the ribbon in a bow, and trim the ends as necessary.

These no-sew desk accessories are easy to make and will brighten up your home office.

MEMORY BOARD

Designed to display favorite photos and cherished mementos, this board needs no sewing skills.

CHECKLIST

Materials

2 coordinating decorator fabrics
Satin ribbon
2 artist's boards
Lightweight quilt batting
Upholstery tacks
Picture-mounting hardware
Paper-backed fusible web and fabric glue
Mat knife and board for cutting

Techniques

Making patterns and cutting
shapes   pp. 16–17
Fusing fabric   pp. 24–25

Measuring up

Measure the width and length of the board.

Cutting sizes

Base Board Use the mat knife to cut one artist's board to the desired size.
Top Board Cut the other artist's board 3in less than the base board in both directions. Trim 1½in off all the corners at a 45-degree angle.
Base Fabric Cut the background fabric 6in greater than the base board in both directions.
Backing Fabric and Fusible Web Cut to the same size as the base board.
Top Fabric Cut this 3in greater than the top board in both directions.
Quilt Batting Cut to the same size as the top board.

1 Place the base fabric wrong side up, and position the base board in the center. Fold one corner of fabric diagonally over the board, and glue it in place. Repeat for the remaining corners.

2 Wrap the straight edges of the fabric to the back of the board, and glue it in place.

3 Following the manufacturer's instructions, apply the fusible web to the wrong side of the backing fabric. Remove the paper backing, and apply the web-backed fabric to the back of the board.

4 Glue the quilt batting to one side of the top board.

5 Lay the top fabric wrong side up, and position the top board, batting side down, in the center. Wrap one corner of the fabric to the back of the board and glue it in place. Repeat for the remaining corners.

6 Wrap the straight edges of the fabric to the back of the board, and glue in place.

7 ► Turn the top board right side up. Cut two pieces of ribbon long enough to reach from one corner to the one diagonally opposite, plus a few inches. Pin the ribbons to the board.

8 ► Cut four more pieces of ribbon, each about two-thirds the length of the first two. Position these ribbons on the board, parallel to the front two, spacing them as shown in the photograph.

9 ► Turn the top board over, and glue the ribbon tails to the back of the board.

10 ► Glue the top board to the center of the base board with right sides facing up.

11 ► Apply glue to the stem of each upholstery tack and push into place at the intersection of the ribbons. Glue the picture-mounting hardware to the back of the board.

Make this memory board in the same fabric as your furniture or draperies to give a coordinated look to your room. If the board is for the office, it could match the desk accessories on page 74.

PADDED PICTURE FRAMES

Economical, colorful frames can easily be made from fabric and pre-cut framing mats.

CHECKLIST

Materials

Decorator fabric
Picture frame mat
Artist's board
Lightweight quilt batting
Narrow ribbon
Paper-backed fusible web
Optional lace trim or piping
Mat knife and cutting board

Techniques

Cutting shapes   pp. 16–17
Fusing fabric   pp. 24–25

Measuring up

Measure the width and length of the pre-cut mat. Measure the inside and outside perimeters of the mat.

Cutting sizes

Base Board The dimensions are identical to those of the mat without the center opening.
Easel Stand The width of the stand is 3in. The length (height of the picture frame) is equal to three-quarters the length of the mat.
Quilt Batting The dimensions are identical to those of the base board.
Fabric Covers and Fusible Web Cut the width and length 4in greater than the base board.
Fabric Easels and Fusible Web Cut the width and length 2in greater than the easel stand.

1 Following the cutting dimensions, cut one base board and one easel stand from artist's board. Cut three fabric covers and two fabric easel pieces. Cut two covers from fusible web and one mat cover from quilt batting. You will also need the purchased mat itself.

2 Place the mat on the quilt batting. Trace the outline of the center opening on the batting, and cut it out. Glue the quilt batting to one side of the mat.

3 Lay one fabric cover wrong side up, and place the mat in the center. Trace the center opening on the fabric.

4 Remove the mat, and draw a line approximately 1in inside the perimeter of the traced opening. Cut the fabric along the inside line, and cut into each of the corners.

5 Lay the fabric wrong side up again, and place the mat, batting side down, on top. Fold and glue the inside edges of the fabric to the wrong side of the mat.

6 Fold each outer corner of fabric diagonally over the mat, and glue it in place.

7 Glue the straight outside edges of the fabric to the wrong side of the mat.

8 Apply optional lace trim or piping to the wrong side of the mat along the inner and outer edges. Glue the header to the mat, and allow the decorative edge to extend over the edge.

9 Following the manufacturer's instructions, apply the fusible web to the remaining two fabric covers. On one cover, trace the perimeter of the base board onto the paper backing. Trim the cover along the traced line.

10▶ Place the base board on the ironing board. Remove the paper backing from the larger cover. Center it, right side up, over the board, and fuse it in place. Avoid taking the iron over the edges.

11▶ Turn the board wrong side up. Fold each outer corner diagonally over the board, and fuse it in place.

12▶ Wrap the straight edges of the fabric to the wrong side of the board, and fuse in place.

13▶ Remove the paper backing from the remaining cover. Place the cover, right side up, on the base board, and fuse it in place.

These no-sew picture frames would make a perfect present for a friend, especially if you use a fabric that matches or tones in with their existing decor.

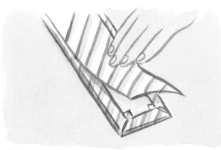

14▶ Apply fusible web to the easel stand pieces. Trim one piece, and cover the stand in the same way as described for the base board in steps 9–13.

15▶ Apply fabric glue to the top 1in of the easel stand. Placing lower

edges together, and centering the stand, glue the stand to the back of the frame. Allow the glue to dry. Glue a 2in-long ribbon between the stand and the frame at the lower edge.

16▶ Apply glue to the lower and side edges of the base board approximately ½in from the edges. Glue the front of the frame to the base. Leave the frame under heavy books overnight to let the glue dry thoroughly. Insert photo between the sections from the top of the frame.

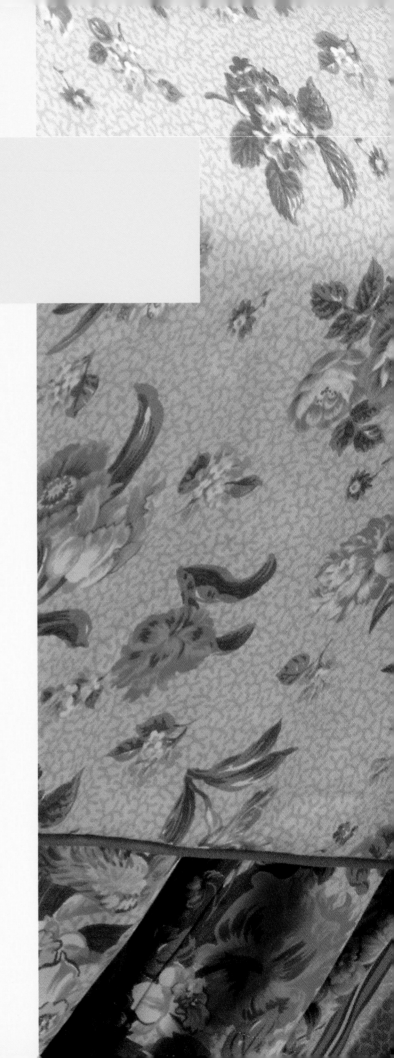

RELAX IN STYLE

The bed is an ideal place to show off your favorite fabric. Cover the bed in one fabric or choose several coordinating fabrics for bed skirt, comforter and pillows. Consider the duvet cover pattern and its companion accessories for true low-sew soft furnishings. Easy to care for sheets, saturated with color are perfect for a child's room. Choose a bed cover style, and a window treatment from the following patterns then mix and match fabrics for a bedroom to be proud of.

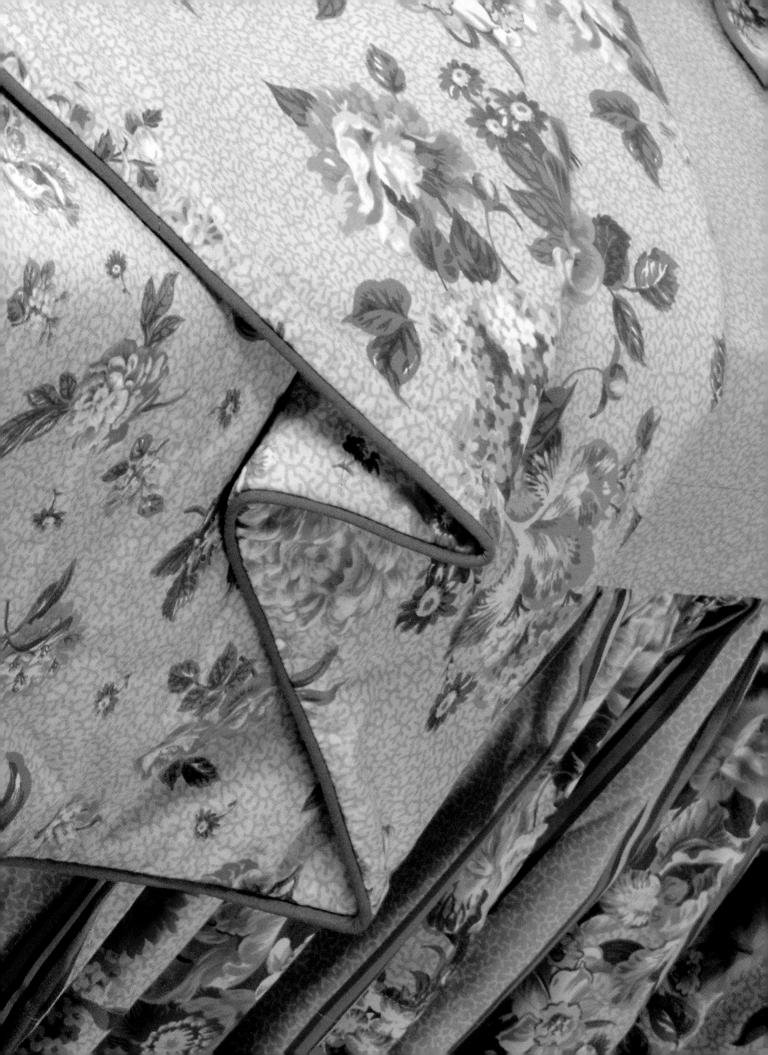

GATHERED BED SKIRT

A pretty striped fabric was chosen for this dust ruffle to create the illusion of height.

C H E C K L I S T

Materials

Decorator fabric
General sewing equipment

Techniques

Measuring up: beds	pp. 12–13
Joining fabric widths	pp. 14–15
Machine stitching	pp. 22–23

Measuring up

Measure the width and length of the box spring. Measure the two lengths plus the width of the box spring for the three-sided perimeter measurement. Measure the drop from the edge of the box spring to the floor.

Cutting sizes

Deck For the cutting width, add 1in to the measured width of the box spring. For the cutting length, add 2½in to the measured length of the box spring.
Skirt For the cutting length of the skirt, multiply the three-sided perimeter measurement by 2½in. For the cutting width of the skirt, add 6in to the measured drop. Piece widths of fabric together if necessary to achieve the cutting dimensions.
The finished skirt will sit ½in above the floor.
Cutting sizes include ½in seam allowance.

1 ▷ Following the cutting dimensions, cut one deck and one skirt. Turn up 2in on the short upper edge of the deck. Tuck the cut edge in to meet the fold and press again. Top stitch the double hem along the inside fold.

2 ▲ Turn under and press 6in on the lower long edge of the skirt. Tuck the cut edge in to meet the fold and press again. Stitch the double hem along the inside fold.

3 ▲ On the short ends of the skirt, turn under and press 2in. Tuck the cut edge in to meet the fold and press again. Stitch the double hem along the inside fold.

4 ▲ Fold the skirt crosswise into four equal sections. Mark the cut edge at the folds with safety pins.

5 ▲ Using one of the recommended gathering methods, work stitching along the cut edge of the skirt section. Start and stop the stitches at the safety pins, leaving long threads. Pull threads (or cord) gently to gather the skirt section.

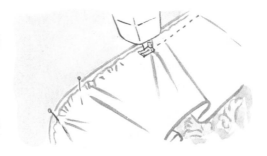

6 Divide the three-sided perimeter of the deck by four to get four equal sections. Mark these distances on the deck edge with safety pins.

7 Matching the safety pin markers, pin the skirt to the deck with right sides together and cut edges matching. Distribute the fullness evenly, and pin the skirt to the deck. Stitch and clean finish the seams.

One continuous ruffle skirts three sides of the bed. Hemming this ruffle could be made easier by using fusible web, if you prefer an iron to a sewing machine.

PIPED BED SET

Commercial piping gives this comforter and pillow sham their tailored styling.

C H E C K L I S T

Materials

Decorator fabric
⅛in-diameter readymade piping
Quilt batting for comforter
Lightweight fusible quilt batting for sham
General sewing equipment

Techniques

Measuring up: beds	pp. 12–13
Joining fabric widths	pp. 14–15
Machine and hand stitching	pp. 22–23
Applying trimmings	pp. 16–17
Fusing fabrics	pp. 24–25

Measuring up

Measure the width and length of the mattress. Determine the desired drop of the comforter from the top edge of the mattress. A drop is equal to the thickness of the mattress plus 6–8in – in this case 15in. For the pillow sham, measure the width and length of the pillow.

Making the pattern

For the comforter:
Cover and Lining For the cutting width, take the width of the mattress and add twice the drop measurement plus 1in. For the cutting length, take the length of the mattress and add the drop measurement plus 1in.

For the pillow sham:
Front For the cutting width and length add 7in to the width and length of the pillow.
Back For the cutting width, add 7in to the width of the pillow. For the cutting length, add the length of the pillow by 2 and add 9½in. Cutting sizes include ½in seam allowance.

To make the comforter:

▶ Following the cutting dimensions, cut one each of the cover, lining, and quilt batting. Piece several widths of fabric together, if necessary, to achieve the cutting dimensions.

▶ To create the rounded corners at the lower end of the comforter cover, use a dinner plate as a template. Position it at the two lower corners, trace around it, and trim the fabric along the lines. Using the cover as a pattern, trim the lining and the batting to match.

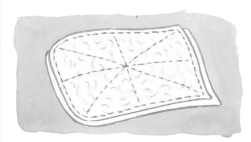

▶ Pin the quilt batting to the wrong side of the cover. Machine baste the layers together ⅜in from all edges. To prevent shifting, especially on a large comforter, hand baste the batting to the comforter cover in a star-burst pattern.

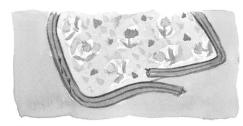

▶ With the cut edges even, pin the piping to the right side of the comforter front along all edges. Cut the ends of the piping so that they overlap slightly.

▶ Using a needle or sharp-pointed scissors, remove the stitches to approximately 1½in from one end of the piping, and fold back the fabric. Trim the covered end and the uncovered end of the cord so that they butt together. Turn under ½in on the edge of the overlapping fabric, and wrap the fabric around the join. Pin the ends together.

▶ Using the sewing machine zipper foot attachment, stitch the piping to the comforter on all edges.

▶ Pin the lining to the cover along all edges placing right sides together. Stitch, leaving an opening of about 20in in one side.

▶ Turn the comforter right side out. Close the opening using slipstitch. Press flat.

9▶ Pin 20 to 30 straight or safety pins to the quilt top at random. At each pin, work several small, nearly invisible hand stitches to hold all the layers together. Remove the star-burst basting stitches.

To make the pillow sham:

10▶ From the decorator fabric, cut one front and two back pieces. From the batting, cut one front. Round off the edges of the sham front following the instructions in step 2. Use the front as a pattern to cut the quilt batting and the sham backs, giving these two rounded outer corners.

11 Pin the quilt batting to the wrong side of the sham front. Fuse the layers together.

12▶ Measure and mark 3½in from all edges of the right side of the sham front.

13▶ Attach the piping to the sham following steps 5–7.

14▶ On the straight inside edge of each back piece, turn under and press 4in. Tuck the cut edge in to meet the fold and press again. Topstitch the double hem along the inside fold.

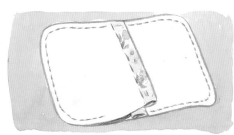

15 Pin the backs to the front with right sides together and cut edges matching, so that the hemmed edges overlap. Using the sewing machine zipper foot attachment, stitch the pieces together along the outer edges.

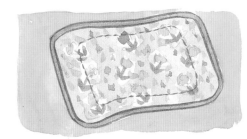

16 Turn the sham right side out. Press flat. Pin all the layers together along the marked line. Check the back of the sham to make sure the hemmed edges are lying flat. Topstitch through all layers along the marked line.

This comforter uses two coordinating decorator fabrics to make a surprising reversible feature. With the large expanse of fabric needed to make a comforter, it is easier to apply the batting with basting, rather than try to fuse it, as is done on the pillow sham.

MOCK PLEAT BED SKIRT

You can make this mock
pleated bed skirt without
pressing a single fold.

CHECKLIST

Materials

2 coordinating decorator fabrics
Fabric for deck and flap lining
General sewing equipment

Techniques

Measuring up: beds	pp. 12–13
Joining fabric widths	pp. 14–15
Machine stitching	pp. 22–23

Measuring up

Measure the width and length of the
box spring. Measure the drop of the skirt
from the box spring to the floor.

Cutting sizes

Determine the width and number of skirt
flaps needed for the sides and the foot of the
bed by dividing the box spring width and
length by 2, 3 or 4, depending upon the size
of the bed. The finished width of the flaps
should measure 16–20 in. The side and foot
flaps may be different widths.
Deck For the cutting width, add 1in to the
box spring width. For the cutting length, add
2½in to the box spring length.
Side and Foot Flaps For the cutting width,
add 1in to the finished width of the flaps.
Under Panels The cutting width of all under
panels is 19in.
For the cutting length of all flaps and panels,
add 1in to the measured drop. The finished
skirt will sit ½in above the floor.
Piece widths of fabric together if necessary to
achieve the cutting dimensions.
Cutting sizes include ½in seam allowance.

1 Cut one deck. Cut the number of
previously determined side flaps, foot
flaps, and under panels, plus a lining
for each.

2 Turn under and press 2in on the
head edge of the deck. Tuck the cut
edge in to meet the fold and press
again. Topstitch the double hem
along the inside fold.

3 Use a large dinner plate as a
template to round off the two corners
at the lower edge of the deck. Place it
on each corner with the edges of the
plate even with fabric edges. Trace
the curve of the plate, and trim the
fabric along the traced line.

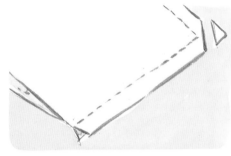

To make a flap or under panel:

4 Pin flap and lining piece together
with right sides facing, and stitch
around the side and lower edges. Trim
the seams and cut across the corners.
Press the seams open.

Note: A slightly larger seam
allowance may be necessary on the
flaps to accommodate the shortened
perimeter of the deck caused by
rounding off the lower corners.

5 Turn the flap right side out, and
press flat. Machine baste the layers
together ⅜in from the edge. Repeat
for all the flaps and under panels.

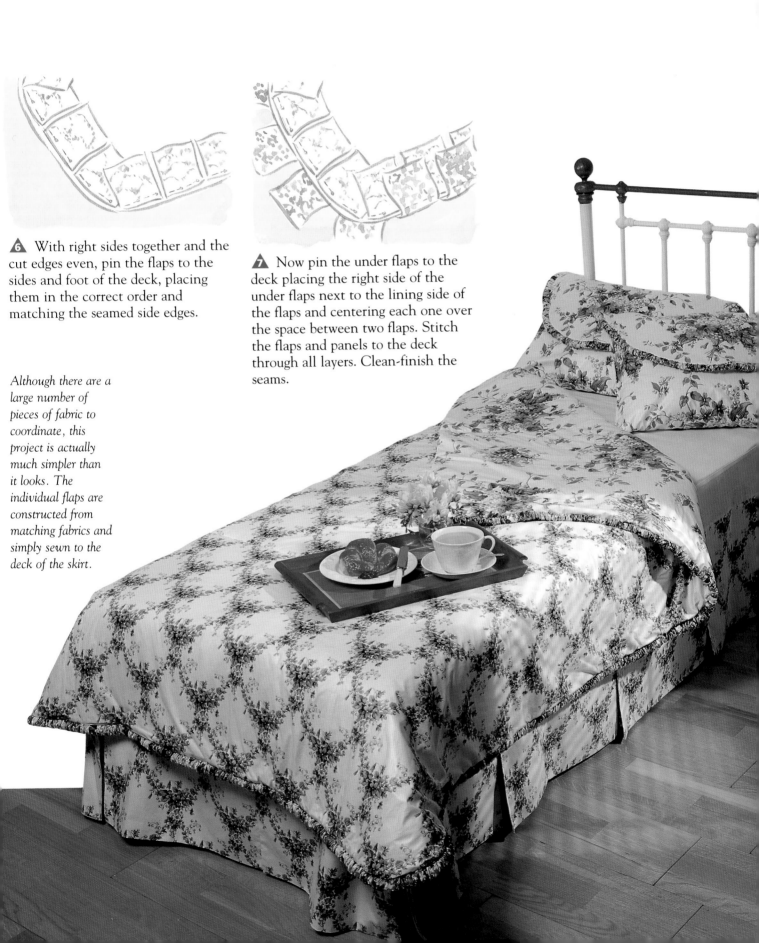

6 With right sides together and the cut edges even, pin the flaps to the sides and foot of the deck, placing them in the correct order and matching the seamed side edges.

Although there are a large number of pieces of fabric to coordinate, this project is actually much simpler than it looks. The individual flaps are constructed from matching fabrics and simply sewn to the deck of the skirt.

7 Now pin the under flaps to the deck placing the right side of the under flaps next to the lining side of the flaps and centering each one over the space between two flaps. Stitch the flaps and panels to the deck through all layers. Clean-finish the seams.

SHIRRED COMFORTER

A custom-made shirred cording adds a contemporary touch to this comforter.

C H E C K L I S T

Materials

3 coordinating decorator fabrics
Quilt batting
1in-wide filler cord
General sewing equipment

Techniques

Measuring up: beds	pp. 12–13
Joining fabric widths	pp. 14–15
Machine stitching	pp. 22–23
Applying trimmings	pp. 16–17
Hand stitching	pp. 22–23

Measuring up

Measure the width and length of the mattress. Determine the desired drop of the comforter from the edge of the mattress. A drop is equal to the thickness of the mattress plus 6–8in – in this case, 15in.

Cutting sizes

Cover and Lining For the cutting width, add twice the drop measurement to the mattress width plus 2in. For the cutting length, add the drop measurement to the mattress length.
Bias Strip for Cording The cutting width is 5in. Add twice the cutting length to the cutting width to get the perimeter around three sides of the comforter. Multiply by 2 to get the cutting length of the strip.
Filler Cord Cut to equal the three-sided perimeter.
Piece several widths of fabric together, if necessary, to achieve the cutting dimensions. Cutting sizes include 1in seam allowance (the extra width simplifies the cording application).

1 ▶ Following the cutting dimensions, cut one main piece each of the cover and lining fabrics. Cut another main piece from batting. Cut and piece the strips for the cording from the third fabrics, following the bias grain.

2 ▶ Use a dinner plate as a template to create the rounded corners at the lower end of the cover piece. Position it at each of the two adjacent corners at one long end. Trace the plate and trim the fabric along the marked lines. Using the cover as a pattern, trim the lining and the batting to match.

3 ▶ Using an erasable pen on the right side of the cover, measure and mark a quilting line 25in from the side and lower edges. Mark additional lines, parallel to the first, if you desire more quilting or if the comforter is very large.

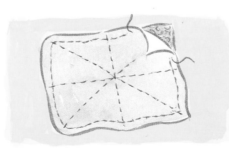

4 ▶ Pin the quilt batting to the wrong side of the cover. Machine baste the layers together ⅜in from all edges. To prevent shifting, especially on a large comforter, hand baste the batting to the comforter cover in a star-burst pattern, using long running stitches.

5 ▶ Fold the bias strip in half lengthwise at each end. Pin and stitch the ends of the strip together. Trim the seam and turn the ends right side out.

6 ▶ Place one end of the filler cord in one end of the strip and secure with a few hand stitches, taking them through the cord and fabric.

7 ▶ Wrap the strip around the cord with the cut edges even. Using the zipper foot on the machine and taking 1in seam allowance, stitch alongside the cord for about 12in. Stop the machine and leave the needle in and the presser foot on the fabric.

8 ▶ Pull gently on the cord, allowing the fabric behind the presser foot to shirr it on. Stitch for another 12in, then stop and shirr the fabric onto

88

the cord. Continue until all the fabric fits on the cord, stopping 6in from the end. Leave the end unstitched for adjustment later. Pin the uncovered cord to the fabric, taking care not to loose the cord end in the shirring. Except for those last few inches, distribute the fullness of the fabric evenly on the cord.

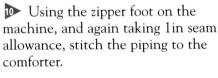

9 Placing the cut edges together, pin the cording to the right side of the comforter along the side and lower edges, beginning and ending 1in from the top edge. At the end, cut the filler cord if necessary to fit the comforter. Sew the cord to the fabric strip as in step 6 to secure. Redistribute the fullness.

10 Using the zipper foot on the machine, and again taking 1in seam allowance, stitch the piping to the comforter.

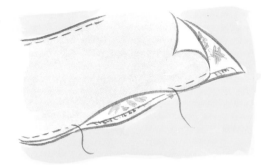

11 Placing right sides together, pin and stitch the lining to the cover along all edges, again taking 1in seam allowance and leaving a 30in opening in one side edge. Trim the seam and cut across the corners.

12 Turn the comforter right side out through the opening. Close the opening edges with slipstitch. Press the edges flat.

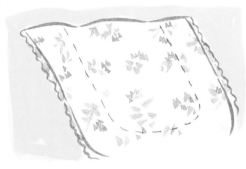

13 Following the marked quilting line, pin and stitch through all the layers. Remove the star-burst basting stitches.

An extra-wide seam allowance is the secret of applying shirred piping. It reduces twisting and simplifies application.

ADULT BEDROOM

The possibilities for a bedroom are enormous. It's a place where you can really allow your imagination to run free. Matching linens, wildly contrasting patterns, or plain colors, traditional, modern, or opulently fantastic – it's your room to furnish exactly to your own taste.

The ruffles and lace are subtly offset in white against the rich cream of the matching linens. Fringes and ribbons give extra texture.

Various types of plaids give a traditional atmosphere. Floral patterns and ruffles soften the straight, geometric lines.

This simple, curved wooden frame produces an exotic, eastern effect. The piles of pillows emphasize this idea.

The small number of colors used in the fabrics unites the varied patterning and prevents it from being uncomfortable to the eye.

QUICK AND EASY QUILT

The quickest way to make an
appealing quilt is by using
cushion panel fabric.

C H E C K L I S T

Materials

Cushion pillow fabric
Fabric for binding and backing
Quilt batting
Contrasting thread for quilting
General sewing equipment

Techniques

Joining fabric widths	pp. 14–15
Cutting the shapes	pp. 16–17
Machine stitching	pp. 22–23
Hand stitching	pp. 22–23

Measuring up

First measure the width and height of one
block of the fabric's design. Also measure the
lattice strips between the blocks. On a sheet
of paper, make a rough sketch of the quilt,
and add up the block and lattice strips
measurements to determine the size of the
visible face of the cover – the main center
section. Be sure to allow for strips around the
outer blocks. Add 1½in to all edges. This is
the finished size – width and height – of the
quilt; record these measurements.

Cutting sizes

Cover Cut two fabric widths, adding ½in to
each for the center seam. Join them, and
press the center seam open.
Batting Cut wadding the same size as cover.
Backing Add 4½in to the visible face
measurements of the cover. Piece widths, as
necessary, to achieve the required size.

1 ▶ Trim the edges of the cover and
backing, if necessary, to make them
the correct sizes.

2 Place the backing wrong side
up on a flat surface and center the
wadding on top. Lay the cover on top
of the wadding, with the edges even.
Pin and hand baste the layers together
in a star-burst pattern.

3 Select the parts of the printed
design that you would like to feature,
and hand quilt all the layers together
along the chosen lines. Use a small,
even-running stitch and ordinary
sewing or quilting thread. The lines
of stitching should be no less than
1in and no more than 12in apart.

4 On all edges, and beginning in
the middle of one side, turn up the
backing 1½in so that the cut edge
meets the batting edge. Turn up 1½in
again, and pin the folded edge of the
backing to the quilt cover. Press the
edges lightly.

5 At each corner, open out the
binding edges and trim off the corner
about 2in from the point. Turn up the
first fold, as in step 4, then fold in the
binding corner diagonally, so that the
fold touches the corner of the
batting and cover fabric.

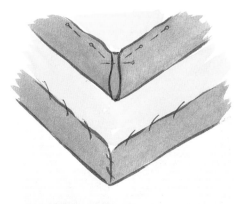

6 Turn up the second fold in the binding so that the diagonal edges meet at the corner, forming a mitered fold. Pin the binding in place.

7 Slipstitch the edges of the binding to the cover, and slipstitch the diagonal corners together.

FINDING THE RIGHT FABRIC

If cushion panel fabric is unavailable, similar results can be achieved with dressmaker or furnishing fabric, or even a sheet, so long as it has a large repeating pattern. Draw a square or rectangle around a selected motif, and add ½in to all edges. If the seam allowances encroach on the next motif, use every other motif. Sew the identical-sized blocks together in strips, then join the strips, and continue with the quilt as instructed.

The most effective quilts are those with strong tonal contrasts and a striking repeated motif which creates the illusion of real patchwork or appliqué.

PINKED PILLOWS

The crisp edges of these pillows
are achieved with fusible web
and a pair of pinking shears.

C H E C K L I S T

Materials

2 coordinated decorator fabrics
Square pillow form
Paper-backed fusible web
General sewing equipment

Techniques

Machine stitching	pp. 22–23
Fusing fabric	pp. 24–25

Measuring up

Measure the width/length of the pillow.

Cutting size

For the cutting size, add 8in to the pillow
form size in both directions.

▶ Following the cutting
dimensions, cut one square from each
of the two fabrics. Cut four rectangles
of fusible web, each 4in wide by the
cutting width/length of the cover.

2▶ Using an air- or water-soluble
pen, measure and mark a 4in border
along all edges on the right side of
the top cover.

3▶ Following the manufacturer's
instructions, apply fusible web to the
wrong side of the top along all edges,
trimming the ends of the web so that
they fit around the square without
overlapping. Remove the paper
backing.

4▶ On the right side of the top,
insert a pin at one marked line.

5▶ Place the top and bottom cover
pieces on the ironing board with
wrong sides together and edges
matching. Fuse together the three
unmarked edges. Do not fuse the
fourth, pinned, edge of the cover.

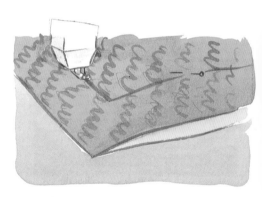

6▶ Stitch the top to the bottom,
following the marked lines on the
fused edges of the cover and
backstitching at the ends to secure.
Do not stitch along the pinned line.

7▶ Remove the marker pin, and
insert the pillow form in the cover
through the opening.

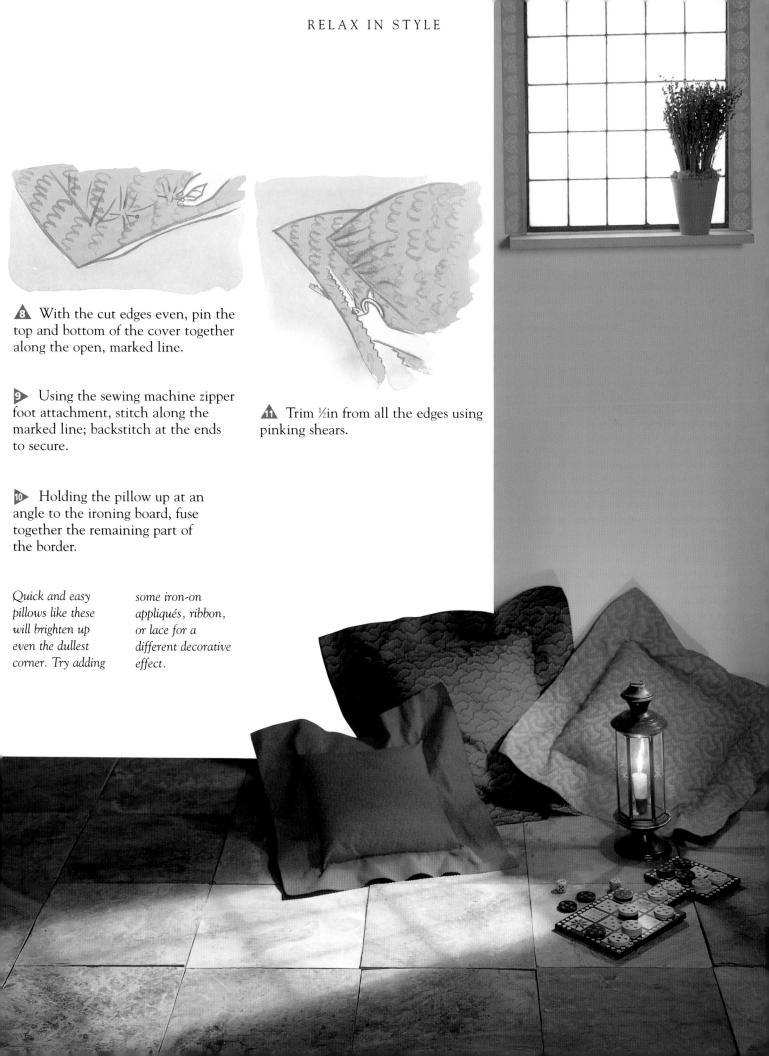

8 With the cut edges even, pin the top and bottom of the cover together along the open, marked line.

9 Using the sewing machine zipper foot attachment, stitch along the marked line; backstitch at the ends to secure.

10 Holding the pillow up at an angle to the ironing board, fuse together the remaining part of the border.

11 Trim ½in from all the edges using pinking shears.

Quick and easy pillows like these will brighten up even the dullest corner. Try adding some iron-on appliqués, ribbon, or lace for a different decorative effect.

TASSEL-VALANCE DRAPERY

The diagonal lines of the valance give these draperies a drama and elegance that would grace a bedroom or living room.

CHECKLIST

Materials

Decorator fabric
Large tassels
General sewing equipment

Techniques

Machine stitching   pp. 22–23

Measuring up

Measure the window frame between its outside edges. Measure the length from the rod to the sill and the rod to the floor. The finished length of the valance will be one-third the distance from the top of the rod to the sill, and the finished length of the drapery will be the distance from the top of the rod to the floor.

Cutting sizes

Drapery Panel For the cutting length, add 4in to the finished length.
Valance For the cutting length, add 2½in to the finished length. For the cutting width of each drapery panel and valance, add 4in to the measured window width.
Piece several widths together, if necessary, to achieve the cutting widths.
The draperies will have a 2 : 1 fullness ratio and will sit ½in above the floor.
Cutting sizes include ½in seam allowance.

To make one panel:

1 At the lower edge of the valance, mark the center point. Draw a line from the mark to each corner at the upper edge of the valance. Cut along the line.

2 Turn under and press 2in on one side edge of the valance. Tuck the cut edge in to meet the fold, and press again. Topstitch the double hem along the inside fold. Repeat for the other side edge.

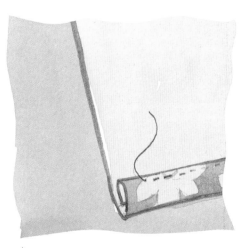

3 Turn under and press 4in on the lower edge of the drapery. Tuck the cut edge in to meet the fold, and press again. Stitch the double hem along the inside fold.

4 Turn under and press 2in on each side edge of the drapery. Tuck the cut edge in to meet the fold, and press again. Topstitch the double hem along the inside fold.

5 Pin the valance to the drapery along the upper edges, with the right side of the valance facing the wrong side of the drapery and the cut edges matching; stitch. Press open and clean-finish the seam.

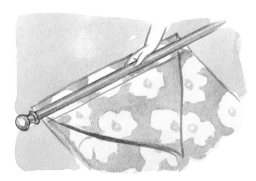

6 Turn the valance over to the right side of the drapery. Press the seam flat. On the right side of the valance, measure and mark 3in, or a dimension equal to the diameter of your drapery rod, plus a little extra for ease, from the seam.

7 Pin and stitch through all the layers along the marked line, backstitching at the ends to secure.

8 Sew a tassel to the point of the valance.

The valance adds an attractive feature to otherwise ordinary curtains. It is simple to make and the addition of a readymade tassel makes it extra special.

To make this an even simpler two-seam project, use fusible web for all of the hemming in steps 2–4.

TAB AND SWAG DRAPERIES

Gauze fabric gives a light and airy feeling to these draperies. The extra-long tabs help to show off a decorative rod.

CHECKLIST

Materials

Coordinating gauze or sheer fabrics
General sewing equipment

Techniques

Joining fabric widths	pp. 14–15
Machine stitching	pp. 22–23
Measuring up: windows	pp. 12–13
Installing window treatments	pp. 12–13

Measuring up

Measure the width of the window frame, between its outside edges, and the length from rod to floor. Use cord to determine the swag length. Drape the cord over the rod at one end, create a swag, and pass it over the rod at the other end. Measure the cord.

Cutting sizes

Drapery Panel For the cutting width, add 4in to the window width. For the cutting length, subtract 2½in from the window length.
Tabs Cut each tab 4 x 22in.
Swag Panel The cutting width equals the fabric width. For the cutting length, add 4in to the cord measurement.
Piece several widths of fabric together, if necessary, to achieve the total panel width. When closed, the drapery will have 2:1 fullness and will hang ½in above the floor. Cutting sizes include ½in seam allowance.

1 Following the cutting dimensions, cut two swag panels, two drapery panels and enough tabs to allow 7–10in spacing between each at the top of the panels.

2 To make the drapery panels: turn under and press 4in on the upper and lower edges of each panel. Tuck the cut edge in to meet the fold and press again. Topstitch the double hem along the inside fold.

3 On the side edge of each panel turn under and press. Tuck the cut edge in to meet the fold and press again. Topstitch the double hem along the inside fold.

To make the tabs:

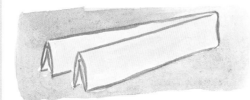

4 Fold the tab in half lengthwise with wrong sides facing, and press. Open up and fold the cut edges so that they meet in the center along the line of the first fold. Now fold this in half again, enclosing the cut edges, and press. Fold the tab in half so that the short edges meet, and stitch close to the folded edges through all eight layers. Repeat for the other tabs.

5 Turn under and press ½in on both ends of the tab. Fold the tab in half crosswise, enclosing the cut ends, and pin the ends together. Repeat for the remaining tabs.

6 Spacing evenly, measure and mark the tab position on the wrong side of the drapery, ½in from the top edge.

7 Matching the hemmed ends to the marked tab positions, pin and stitch the tabs to the wrong side of the drapery at the upper edge.

To make the swag panels:

8▶ On the two long edges of the swag panel, turn under and press 2in. Tuck the cut edge in to meet the fold and press again. Stitch along the second fold.

9 On the two short ends of the panel, turn under and press 2in. Tuck the cut edge in to meet the fold and press again. Stitch close to the second fold.

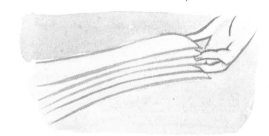

10 In a large room or a long hallway, fold the panel lengthwise in soft, accordion-style pleats approximately 9in wide. The two long hemmed edges should begin and end at the same side of the folded stack. Do not press the pleats.

11▶ For very long swags, pin the stack together with extra-large safety pins. Carry the fabric to the window and drape it over the rod in the same fashion as the cord, with the long hemmed edges facing the wall.

This graceful window dressing, which is achieved without the use of drapery hooks, will add elegance to any room. The sewing could be reduced by using fusible web to hem the drapery and swag panels.

PILLOW-TOPPED OTTOMAN

Make this slipcover to improve upon an existing ottoman or cover a wooden box for quick and easy furniture.

CHECKLIST

Materials

Decorator fabric
Quilt batting
General sewing equipment

Techniques

Joining fabric widths	pp. 14–15
Machine stitching	pp. 22–23

Measuring up

Measure the width and length of the ottoman and the height from the top edge to the floor.

Cutting sizes

Top For the cutting width and length, add 1in to the width and length of the ottoman.
Side skirt pieces For the cutting length, add 17in to the measured length.
End skirt pieces For the cutting length, add 17in to the measured width. For the cutting width of all skirts, add 2in to the height of the ottoman.
NOTE: If the ottoman is square, all four skirt pieces will be the same width.
Pillow For the cutting width and length, add 3in to the width and length of the ottoman.
Pillow Ties Cut each pillow tie 3 x 12in.
The finished skirt will sit ½in above floor.
Cutting sizes include ½in seam allowance.

1 Following the cutting dimensions, cut one top; two each of skirt sides, skirt ends, and pillow; and eight pillow ties.

2 With right sides together, stitch the sides and ends of the skirt together, alternating sides and ends to create one continuous loop of fabric. Press all of the seams open and clean-finish the edges.

3 Clean-finish the one long edge of the skirt. Turn under and press 2in on this edge. Sew the hem in place by hand or machine.

4 Locate each of the seams joining the skirt sections. On the right side of the fabric, measure and mark parallel lines 4in and 8in to each side of each seam.

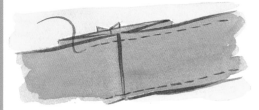

5 Matching the marks, press an inverted pleat at each seam. Machine or hand baste the pleat ¼in from the cut edge.

6 Turn under and press ½in on one short end of one tie. Turn under and press ½in on the two side edges.

7 Fold the tie in half lengthwise with wrong sides and folded edges together. Topstitch close to the fold along the long and short edges. Repeat steps 6 and 7 for all ties.

8 Mark the mid-point of each edge of the ottoman top. With the cut edges even, pin and stitch a tie to each mark on the right side of the fabric.

9 Pin the skirt to the ottoman top, placing right sides together and matching the pleats with the corners.

To simplify turning the corners, cut diagonally across the corners, and clip the pleat at the seamline up to the basting stitches. Stitch the seam, taking care not to catch the loose ends of the ties in the seam. Clean-finish the seam edges.

To make the pillow:

10 ▶ Mark the mid-point of each edge on one pillow piece. Pin and stitch a tie to each mark on the right side of the pillow, placing cut edges together.

11 ▶ Place the two pillow pieces together with right sides facing. Pin and stitch around the edges, leaving almost all of one edge open. Avoid catching the loose ends of the ties in the seam.

12 ▶ Turn pillow right side out. Cut two pieces of quilt batting the same size as the pillow and two more pairs, grading each pair to be 2in smaller than the previous size. Place all six layers together, with the smallest pieces at the top and bottom and larger pieces in the center. Loosely baste the batting layers together.

13 ▶ Insert the batting into the pillow cover, and close the opening with slipstitch.

14 ▶ Attach the pillow to the top of the ottoman cover by tying each pair of ties in a square knot.

Inverted pleats at the four corners give a crisply tailored look to this ottoman slipcover.

DUVET COVER

Only two bed sheets, three seams and a few buttonholes are needed to complete a cozy duvet cover.

CHECKLIST

Materials

2 bed sheets
5 large buttons
Purchased duvet
General sewing equipment

Techniques

Measuring up: beds	pp. 12–13
Machine stitching	pp. 22–23

Measuring up

Measure the width and length of the duvet. Measure the width of the mattress add twice the depth of the mattress plus 14in. Measure the length of the mattress plus the drop at the foot of the bed; add the depth of the mattress plus 7in.

Cutting sizes

Top (A) For the cutting width, add 1in to the measured width of the mattress.
For the cutting length, subtract 4½in from the measured length.
Bottom (B) For the cutting width, add 1in to the measured width.
For the cutting length, add 10½in to the measured length.
Purchase sheets wide enough to accommodate the cutting width of the cover. Cutting sizes include ½in seam allowance.

1 Measuring from the hemmed edge of each sheet, mark the cutting length for the top and bottom pieces. Measure and mark the cutting width for each cover piece. Cut along marked lines.

2 On the bottom, fold 10in to the right side along the hemmed edge. Do not press the fold. Machine baste the side edges together.

3 Pin the top cover to the bottom cover with right sides facing and cut edges even, so that the top overlaps the turned-over-edge of the bottom piece. Stitch the three cut edges together. Clean-finish the seams.

4 Turn the cover right side out. The sheet hem from the bottom cover now appears on the front in an envelope-style flap. Along the center of the hem, measure 20in from each side edge and mark a buttonhole position. Mark three more buttonholes between these two, spacing them evenly and centering them in the hem. Stitch buttonholes in the hem of the cover.

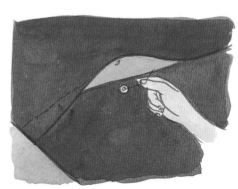

5 Using pins, mark the button position below each buttonhole on the hidden sheet hem of the cover top. Sew buttons to the hem of the cover top.

FLANGED PILLOW SHAM

A pillow is neatly dressed in a ribbon-trimmed pillow sham which features an envelope-style back opening.

CHECKLIST

Materials

Bed sheet
Fusible interfacing
⅞in-wide grosgrain ribbon
General sewing equipment

Techniques

Machine stitching	pp. 22–23
Applying trimmings	pp. 16–17

Measuring up

Measure the width and length of the pillow.

Cutting sizes

Front (A) For the cutting width and length, add 7in to the measured width and length of the pillow.
Back (B) For the cutting width, add 7in to the width of the pillow. For the cutting length, take half the measured length and add 9¼in. Depending upon the pillow size, the cutting width may now exceed the length.
Cutting sizes include ½in seam allowance.

1 Cut one front and two back pieces from the sheet and one front piece from the interfacing.

2 Measure and mark 3½in from all edges of the sham front on the right side of the fabric. Fuse the ribbon to sham front along the inside edge of the marked line, folding in mitered corners and turning under the cut ends to clean-finish.

3 Fuse the interfacing to the wrong side of the sham front.

4 Lay the two back pieces on the interfaced side of the front piece so that cut edges match and the two inner edges of the back piece overlap. Lift up each piece separately and, on one inner edge, turn under and press

4in. Tuck the cut edge in to meet the fold and press again. Topstitch the double hem along the inside fold.

5 Reassemble the pieces as in step 4, and pin them together. Stitch the pieces together along all edges. Cut across the corners and press the seams open.

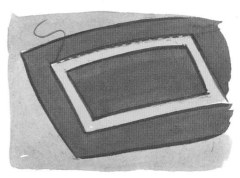

6 Turn the sham right side out through the hemmed opening, and press flat. Pin all the layers together along the applied ribbon. Check the back of the sham to make sure that the flaps are lying flat. Topstitch through all layers along the outer edge of ribbon.

PLEATED BED SKIRT

Inverted pleats are featured at the sides and lower corners of this low-sew bed skirt.

CHECKLIST

Materials

Bed sheets
⅞in-wide grosgrain ribbon
General sewing equipment

Techniques

Measuring up: beds	pp. 12–13
Joining fabric widths	pp. 14–15
Machine stitching	pp. 22–23
Applying trimmings	pp. 16–17

Measuring up

Measure the width and length of the mattress. Measure the drop from the bottom edge of the mattress to the floor.

Cutting sizes

Deck For the cutting width, add 1in to the measured width of the mattress. For the cutting length, add 2½in to the measured length.
Upper Skirt For the cutting length of the skirt at the upper sides of the bed, take half the measured length of the mattress and add 10½in.
Lower Skirt For the cutting length of the skirt at the lower sides of the bed, take half the measured length and add 17in.
Foot Skirt For the cutting length of the skirt at the foot of the bed, add 17in to the measured width.
All skirts For the cutting width, add 4in to the measured drop. Piece several widths of fabric together if necessary to achieve the cutting dimensions. The finished skirt will sit ½in above the floor.
Cutting sizes include ½in seam allowance.

1 Cut one deck, one foot skirt, and two each of upper, lower. Stitch the upper side, lower side, and foot sections of the skirt together in the correct order, matching the short edges and placing right sides together. Press the seams open and clean finish the edges.

2 On each short end of the skirt, turn under and press 2in. Tuck the cut edge in to meet the fold and press again. Topstitch the double hem along the inside fold.

3 On the lower, long edge of the skirt, turn under and press 4in. Tuck the cut edge in to meet the fold and press again. Topstitch the double hem along the upper fold. Stitch or fuse the ribbon along the hem, following the stitching line, and turn under ½in at each end to clean-finish.

4 Locate each of the seams joining the upper, lower and foot skirt sections. On the right side of the fabric, measure and mark two parallel lines 4in and 8in to each side of every seam.

8 Pin the bed skirt to the side and foot edges of the deck, placing right sides and cut edges together, and positioning the pleats at the lower corners and midway along the sides. Stitch and clean-finish the seams.

5 Fold the fabric along the outer marked lines, wrong sides together; press. Then bring the folds together at the seam and press again, including the inner folds, to make an inverted pleat. Baste the pleat ¼in from the cut edge.

By using bed sheets for fabric, you can eliminate the task of piecing together many fabric widths.

7 To round off the two corners at the lower edge of the deck, place a large dinner plate on the corner, aligning it with the fabric edges. Trace the curve of the plate, and trim the fabric along the traced line.

6 Turn under and press 2in on the head edge of the deck. Tuck the cut edge in to meet the fold and press again. Topstitch the double hem along the inside fold.

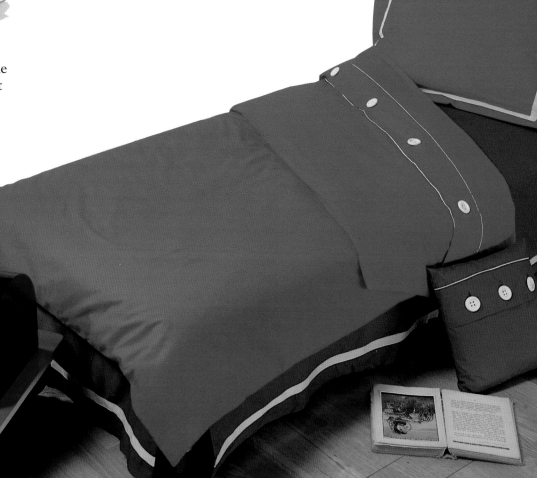

ROPE-TRIMMED CURTAIN

On this curtain, cotton cord looped over a rod is an important element of the design.

CHECKLIST

Materials

Decorator fabric
Twisted cord
Metal eyelets
Fusible interfacing
General sewing equipment

Techniques

Joining fabric widths	pp. 14–15
Machine stitching	pp. 22–23
Fusing fabric	pp. 24–25

Measuring up

Measure the width and length of the window frame between outside edges and sill. For a shower curtain, measure the width and length of the area to be covered above the bathtub. Standard shower curtains usually measure 70in square.

Cutting sizes

Curtain Panel For the cutting width, add 12in to the measured width of window. For the cutting length, add 4½in to the measured length.
Heading The cutting width is 9in. For the length, add 2in to the measured width. Piece several widths of fabric together if necessary to achieve the total curtain width. When closed, the curtain will hang flat. Cutting sizes include ½in seam allowance.

1 Following the cutting dimensions, cut one curtain panel and one heading. Also cut one heading from interfacing.

2 Turn under and press 8in on the lower edge of the curtain. Tuck cut edge in to meet the fold. Press. Topstitch double hem along inside fold.

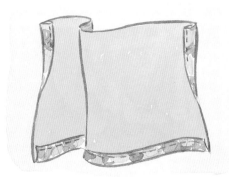

3 Turn under and press 6in on the side edges of the curtain. Tuck the cut edge in to meet the fold and press again. Topstitch the double hem along the inside fold.

4 Following the manufacturer's instructions, fuse the interfacing to the wrong side of the heading. Turn under and press ½in on one long edge of the heading.

5 Pin the heading to the curtain right sides together, matching the long cut edges. The heading extends ½in beyond the hemmed sides of the curtain. Stitch. Press seam allowances toward the heading.

6 Turn the fabric right side up. Bring the edge of the heading down to the stitching line, thus folding the heading in half. Pin the ends together. Using a ruler and the curtain edges as guides, mark the stitching line. Stitch seams; cut across the corners diagonally.

7 Turn the heading right side out. On the wrong side of the curtain, pin the fold of the heading along the stitching line. Topstitch through all layers along the fold.

8▶ Mark the eyelets' positions on the right side of the heading, spacing them 4–6in apart. The first and last eyelet should be placed either 1½in from the side edge or in the center of the side hem. Fix the metal eyelets to the curtain.

9▶ Tie a knot 2in from one end of the cord, to prevent it from raveling, and tie another 18in from it. To determine the distance between knots, lay the curtain flat and position the rod the desired distance above it. Using a tape measure, measure the distance from one eyelet to the next, over the rod. Check the amount of cord taken up by a knot, and add this to the spacing measurement. Mark this total measurement along the cord the required number of times for the

eyelets (subtracting the knot measurement for the mark following the already tied knot).

10▶ Thread the cord through the first eyelet, from front to back, then through the second. Tie a knot just

after the first mark. Continue in this way until you have a knot at each eyelet.

11▶ After the last eyelet, tie a knot 18in along the cord. Cut the cord 2in beyond this knot. Fluff out the cord ends on the first and last knots.

The cord and metal eyelets give this stylish curtain an extra boost.

Select a striped fabric and use it creatively at the heading of the curtain. Experiment with eyelet and cord sizes to find the right fit. This design is ideal for use in a child's bedroom. It could also make a perfect shower curtain if teamed with a plastic liner.

QUILTED COMFORTER

Bright pastels make this channel-quilted comforter an eye-catcher.

C H E C K L I S T

Materials

Decorator fabric
Lining fabric
Quilt batting
1in-wide double-fold quilt binding
General sewing equipment

Techniques

Measuring up: beds	pp. 12–13
Joining fabric widths	pp. 14–15
Machine stitching	pp. 22–23
Applying trimmings	pp. 16–17
Hand stitching	pp. 22–23

Measuring up

Measure the width and length of the mattress. Determine the desired drop of the quilt from the edge of the mattress. A drop is equal to the thickness of the mattress plus 6–8in. For this quilt it measures 15in.

Cutting sizes

Cover and Lining For the cutting width, multiply the drop measurement by 2; add the mattress width plus 1in. For the cutting length, add the drop measurement to the mattress length plus 1in.
Piece several widths of fabric together, if necessary, to achieve the cutting dimensions.
Cutting sizes include ½in seam allowance.

1 Following the cutting dimensions, cut one piece each of the cover, lining and quilt batting.

2 To determine how many quilting lines you will need, divide the cutting width of the quilt by 8. On the right side of the cover and using a yardstick and water-soluble pen, measure and mark quilting lines lengthwise on the cover, parallel with the side edges.

3 Use a dinner plate as a template for the rounded corners at the lower end of the quilt. Position it at each of the two adjacent corners at one long end of the quilt cover, and trace around it. Trim the fabric along the lines. Using the quilt cover as a pattern, trim the lining and batting pieces at the lower corners only.

4 Pin the batting to the wrong side of the cover. Machine baste the layers together ⅜in from all edges.

5 With right sides facing, pin and hand or machine stitch the cover to the lining at the short upper edge.

6 Trim the batting from the seam allowance on the stitched edge, and press the seam open. Turn the quilt right side out, so that the batting lies between the fabric layers.

7 On the upper edge, pin and topstitch the layers together 1in from the seamline. Pin the layers together on the side and lower edges.

8 Hand- or pin-baste the layers of the quilt together along the marked lines.

9▶ Machine stitch through all layers along the marked lines, beginning each time at the seamed upper edge and ending at the lower edge.

10 Piece the quilt binding along the straight grain, as follows. First open out the folds. Place two ends together with right sides facing to form a right angle. Mark a straight line at a 45-degree angle across the corner. Stitch the binding strips together along the line. Trim ¼in from the stitching line, cutting off the corner.

11▶ Press the seam open, and re-press the manufacturer's folds. Piece together enough quilt binding to equal the length of both sides plus the lower edge of the quilt.

Commercial quilt binding in a coordinating color – a quick alternative to hand-cut binding – is applied to the edges of this quilt.

12. On one end of the binding, turn under and press ½in side. Pin the quilt binding around the side and lower edges of the quilt top, placing right sides together and aligning the outer binding crease with the seamline.

13▶ Stitch the binding to the quilt through all layers along the crease of the binding.

14▶ Turn and pin the binding to the wrong side of the quilt, enclosing the cut edge of the quilt. Slipstitch the binding to the lining along edges.

RUFFLED PILLOW SHAM

Ruffles frame a pillow sham designed to coordinate with the quilt and dust ruffle.

C H E C K L I S T

Materials

2 coordinating decorator fabrics
General sewing equipment

Techniques

Joining fabric widths   pp. 14–15
Machine stitching   pp. 22–23

Measuring up

Measure the width and length of the bed pillow. Add these measurements together and multiply by 2 to get the perimeter.

Cutting sizes

Front (A) For the cutting width and length, add 1in to the width and length of the pillow.
Back (B) For the cutting width, add 1in to the width of the pillow. For the cutting length, divide the pillow length by 2 and add 6½in.

Note: Depending upon the pillow size, the cutting width of the back pieces may exceed the length.
Ruffle (C) The cutting width is 9in. For the cutting length, multiply the perimeter by 2½. Cutting sizes include ½in seam allowance.

1 ▶ From the main decorator fabric, cut one front and two back pieces. From the other fabric, cut one ruffle following the bias grain of the fabric. You will probably need to piece several strips together to achieve the cutting length for the ruffle.

2 ▶ Stitch the short ends of the ruffle together with right sides facing to form a continuous loop. Press the seams open.

3 ▶ Fold the ruffle in half lengthwise with wrong sides facing; press the fold. Pin the long cut edges together.

4 ▶ Fold the ruffle in half crosswise, then in half again to divide it into four equal sections. Mark the sections along the cut edge.

5 ▶ Using one of the recommended methods, stitch gathering threads along the cut edges of each of the four sections separately. Pull the threads gently to gather the skirt section.

6 ▶ By folding crosswise and lengthwise, divide the pillow front into four equal sections. Mark at the cut edges.

7 ▶ Matching the markings and placing cut edges together, pin the ruffle to the right side of the pillow front.

MAKING A MATCHING BED SKIRT

The perfect complement to this bed set, intended for a young girl, is a ruffled bed skirt. The simple assembly is almost the same as that used for the gathered bed skirt on page 82. The only difference is that the sides and lower edge of this bed skirt were hemmed and gathered separately before being sewn to the deck.

8 Pull the threads to gather the edge of the ruffle. Distributing the fullness evenly, pin all the edges of the ruffle to the pillow front. Machine baste the ruffle to the front ⅜in from the edges.

9 Turn under and press 4 in on one "width" edge of each back piece. Tuck the cut edge in to meet the fold and press again. Topstitch the double hem along the inside fold.

10 Pin the backs to the ruffled front, placing right sides and cut edges together and overlapping the hemmed edges of the back pieces at the center. Stitch the pieces together along all outer edges. Trim the seam and cut across the corners.

11 Turn the sham right side out through the hemmed opening. Insert the pillow.

The width of the ruffle adds an extra dimension to the pillow.

The complementary patterns provide flair and interest.

The variation in color of pillow and ruffle give more choice when making up a matching set.

BUTTERFLY VALANCE

In a matter of minutes, transform two lace-trimmed bed sheets into a pretty butterfly valance.

C H E C K L I S T

Materials

2 twin bed sheets with decorative hems
3¾yd of 1½in-wide ribbon
3¾yd of fusible 2-cord shirring tape
Fusible web strip ⅜in wide
Hook and loop tape
General sewing equipment
Fabric glue
Mounting board and hardware

Techniques

Measuring up: windows   pp. 12–13
Installing window treatments   pp. 12–13

Measuring up

Measure the width of the window frame between its outside edges. Measure the length of the window.

Cutting sizes

Swag and right tail Divide the window width by 8; subtract one-eighth for the left tail. To the remainder, add one-third of the window length, which is the tail length. The total is the cutting length of the swag and right tail.
Left tail Add the tail length (one-third window length) to one-eighth of the window width. This is the cutting length. The piecing seam joining these two pieces will be concealed by the shirring and ribbon. For a very wide window it may be necessary to use three sheets and piece the right-hand side of the valance also.
Cutting sizes include ½in seam allowances.

1 Measuring from the decorative hemmed edge of each sheet, mark the cutting length for the swag and right tail on one sheet and the cutting length for the left tail on the other. Cut across each sheet on these lines.

2 Turn under and press the seam allowance on the tail piece. Cut a piece of fusible web to fit. Placing the folded tail edge over the swag edge, right sides upward, and positioning the web in between, fuse them together.

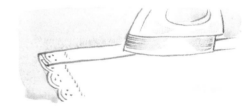

3 The next step is optional, depending on how well the sheet is hemmed. Turn under and press 1in on each long edge. Tuck the cut edge in to meet the fold. Fuse each double hem along the inside fold.

4 Fold the valance in half down the middle of the swag, with right sides together. Lay it on a flat surface, seamed side down. Pin the two layers together along the seam and, using an erasable pen, trace the seamline onto the swag and tail piece. This marks the position for the shirring tape.

This luxurious valance looks far more complex than it really is; in fact it is totally "no sew." Fusible web and shirring tape remove the need to set up the sewing machine or even thread a needle.

5 Cut two pieces of shirring tape long enough to reach from the top to the bottom of the valance. Center the tape on the seam and the marked line on the wrong side, and fuse it in place. To gather the valance, pull up the cords and tie them together.

6 Cut a piece of hook and loop tape equal to the window width. Glue the loop (fuzzy) half to the top edge of the valance on the wrong side, centering it between the two ends.

7 Staple or glue the hook (stiff) half of the tape to the long back edge on top of the mounting board.

8 Position the valance on the mounting board and join the hook and loop tapes. Cut the ribbon in two. Slip each piece of ribbon between the hook and loop tape at the top of the shirring, and tie it in a bow. Trim the ends as required.

SIMPLE SHOWER CURTAIN

Extra-wide fabric printed with large blocks is a perfect choice for a decorative shower curtain.

CHECKLIST

Materials

Decorator fabric
Paper-backed ⅜in-wide fusible web strip
General sewing equipment

Techniques

Joining fabric widths	pp. 14–15
Machine stitching	pp. 22–23
Fusing fabric	pp. 24–25

Measuring up

Measure the width and length of the bathtub opening from the rod to halfway down the sides of the tub. Standard shower curtains usually measure 70in square.

Cutting sizes

Curtain For the cutting width, add 4in to the measured width of the bathtub opening. For the cutting length, add 4in to the measured length.
Tabs Cut each tab 4 x 9 in.
Piece several widths of fabric together if necessary to achieve the total curtain width. When closed, the curtain will hang flat with no fullness.
Cutting sizes include ½in seam allowance.

1 ▶ Following the cutting dimensions, cut one curtain and enough tabs to allow a 7–10in spacing between each at the top of the curtain.

2 ▶ Turn under and press 2in on the upper and lower edges of the curtain. Tuck the cut edge in to meet the fold, and press again. Topstitch the double hem along the inside fold. Repeat for the side edges.

3 ▶ Turn under and press ½in on both long edges of each tab. Following the manufacturer's instructions, apply fusible web to the seam allowance of one edge. Remove the paper backing.

4 ▶ Bring over the other edge – with the seam allowance still folded in – to meet the edge with the web. Fuse the two edges together, and press flat.

5 ▶ Fold the tab in half crosswise, and pin the ends together.

6 ▶ Spacing evenly, measure and mark each tab position on the wrong side of the curtain 1in from the top edge.

7 ▶ Matching the cut ends to the tab positions, pin and sew the tabs to the wrong side of the curtain at the upper edge.

Here are some easy and attractive alternatives to the standard tab shower curtain.
—Replace fabric tabs with extra-wide grosgrain ribbon.
—Select wide eyelet trim for tab tops.
—Cut each ribbon tab 36in long. Fold in half and sew the folded end to the curtain along the upper and lower edges of the hem. Tie the ribbon tails into a bow.

All four edges of this curtain are simply hemmed by either topstitching or fusing them in place. Construct the tabs by fusing the seam, but sew them to the curtain for added security. Team the shower curtain with a purchased plastic liner to keep it dry.

RUCHED RIBBON TOWEL

For a stylish bathroom, trim plain towels by sewing on wide ribbon and twisted cord.

CHECKLIST

Materials

Bath towel
Wide ribbon or !ace
Twisted cord

Techniques

Machine stitching   pp. 22–23

Measuring up

Measure the width of the towel.

1 Cut two pieces of ribbon equal to half the measured width of the towel plus 1in. Cut two lengths of cord equal to half the measured width of the towel plus 12in.

2 On one end of each ribbon, turn under and press 1in. Tuck the cut edge in to meet the fold and press again. Sew the second fold in place by hand or machine.

3 On the other ends, turn under and press ½in.

4 Pin the two pieces of ribbon to the towel, covering the transition border and placing the pressed, unstitched ends even with the sides. There should be a gap of about 1in at the center. Stitch the long edges, backstitching at the inside ends to secure. This type of stitching is much quicker by machine.

5 On the outside ends, measure and mark the ribbon ½in from the fold. Attach a safety pin to one end of a twisted cord. Insert the cord into the casing formed by the ribbon until the end of the cord is even with the side edge of the towel. Following the marked line, stitch the ribbon to the towel through the cord, backstitching in the area of the cord to secure. Trim the cord ¼in from the end. Repeat for the remaining cord.

6 Sew the ribbon ends to the towel along the outside fold.

7 Pull the cords gently to gather the towel. Tie the cords into a bow and knot the cord ends.

If you mix and match ribbon and cord, the possibilities are endless. By adding the same trimmings to the curtains or vanity skirt in your bathroom you could create a beautifully co-ordinated effect.

BEACH BLANKET

Transform an ordinary blanket into something special by adding a coordinating fabric border.

C H E C K L I S T

Materials

Decorator fabric featuring printed motifs
Blanket
General sewing equipment
Paper-backed fusible web

Techniques

Machine stitching	pp. 22–23
Hand stitching	pp. 22–23
Fusing fabrics	pp. 24–25

Measuring up

Measure the width and length of the blanket.

Cutting sizes

Side Borders For the cutting length, add 1in to the length of the blanket.
End Borders For the cutting length, add 1in to the width of the blanket.
All Borders The cutting width is 11in. Piece several fabric widths together, if necessary, to achieve the cutting lengths. Cutting sizes include ½in seam allowance.

1 Following the cutting dimensions, cut two side borders and two end borders.

2 Cut several motifs from the fabric, allowing a margin of at least ½in around the motif and making straight cuts, rather than attempting to follow the shapes closely. Place fusible web, paper side up, over the wrong side of each motif, and trace the cut edges. Cut the shape from the web. Pin each motif and the corresponding web shape together and set aside.

3 On the right side of the blanket mark a line 4½in from the edge on all sides.

4 Turn under and press ½in on one long edge of each border piece. On the other long edge, on the wrong side of the fabric, mark a stitching line ½in from the edge.

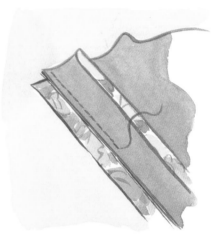

5 Pin one side border to one side edge of the blanket, right sides together, placing the unfolded edge on the marked line and the folded edge toward the center of the blanket. Allow the border ends to overlap the top and bottom edges of the blanket by ½in. Following the stitching line on the border, stitch it to the blanket. Repeat with the other side border.

6 Fold in the short ends of the borders even with the top and bottom edges of the blanket. Then fold each border in half lengthwise over the side edges of the blanket, matching the long folded edge to the line of stitching on the wrong side of the blanket. Topstitch through all layers, or use slipstitch to sew the folded edge in place.

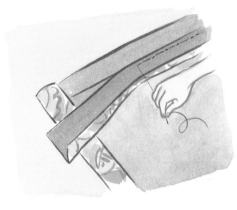

7 Pin the two end borders to the top and bottom edges of the blanket, in the same way as for the side border. Allow ½in of the border to extend past the edge of the blanket. Following the stitching line, stitch the borders in place, beginning and ending with backstitching at the inner corners where the adjacent borders meet.

8 Fold in the ends of the border even with the side edges of the blanket. Fold the borders over the

edges of the blanket, matching the long folded edge to the line of stitching on the wrong side of the blanket. Topstitch through all layers, or use slipstitch to sew the folded edge in place, beginning and ending at the inner corners where the borders meet.

9 On the right side, tuck under the points of the end borders to create a mitered corner. The fold should extend from the outer to the inner corner. Trim the point if necessary to reduce bulk. Repeat on the wrong side of the blanket.

10 Slipstitch the fold in place on the right and wrong sides of the border.

Select interesting motifs from the fabric and apply them using fusible web.

To complete the appliqués:

11 Following the manufacturer's instructions, iron each fusible web piece to the wrong side of the corresponding motif. Trim the appliqué carefully along the edge of the motif. Remove the paper backing, and apply the motifs to the blanket.

To make a whole beach ensemble, fuse some of these motifs to a beach umbrella or onto the picnic basket on page 34.

TEMPLATES

The templates in the following pages can be used for the appliqué shapes required for the Appliquéd picnic basket (page 34), the Pillowcase café curtains (page 40), and the Beach blanket (page 118). Or use your own designs. Each needs to be applied with paper-backed fusible web. This can be used in different ways (see the individual project instructions).

Note that you will need to make separate tracings for the leaves and for the shaded parts of the Beach blanket motifs. These can then be applied on top of the complete shape. If the design needs to be enlarged or reduced, use either a larger or smaller grid than the one here, and transfer the designs accordingly.

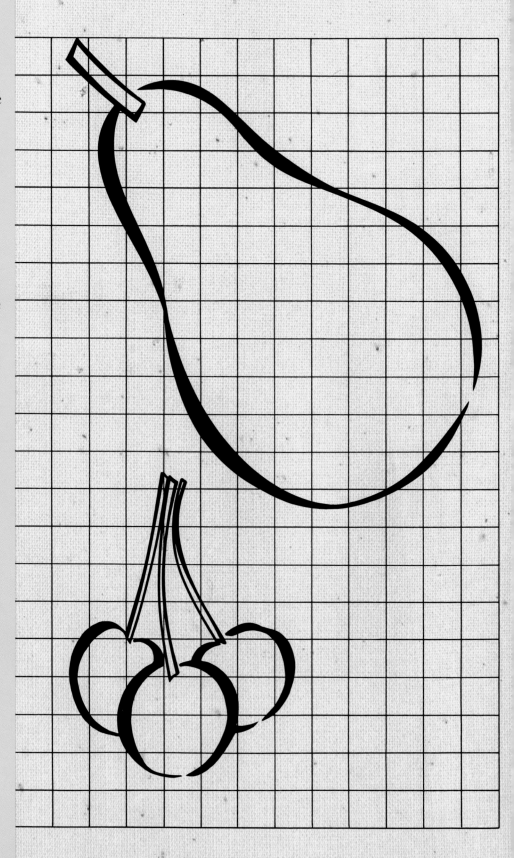

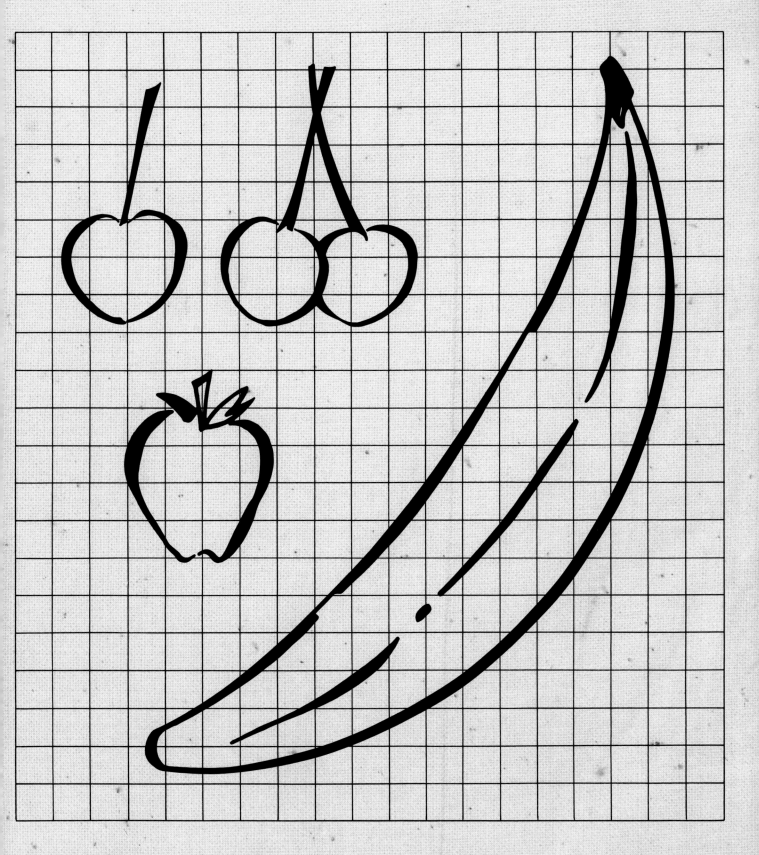

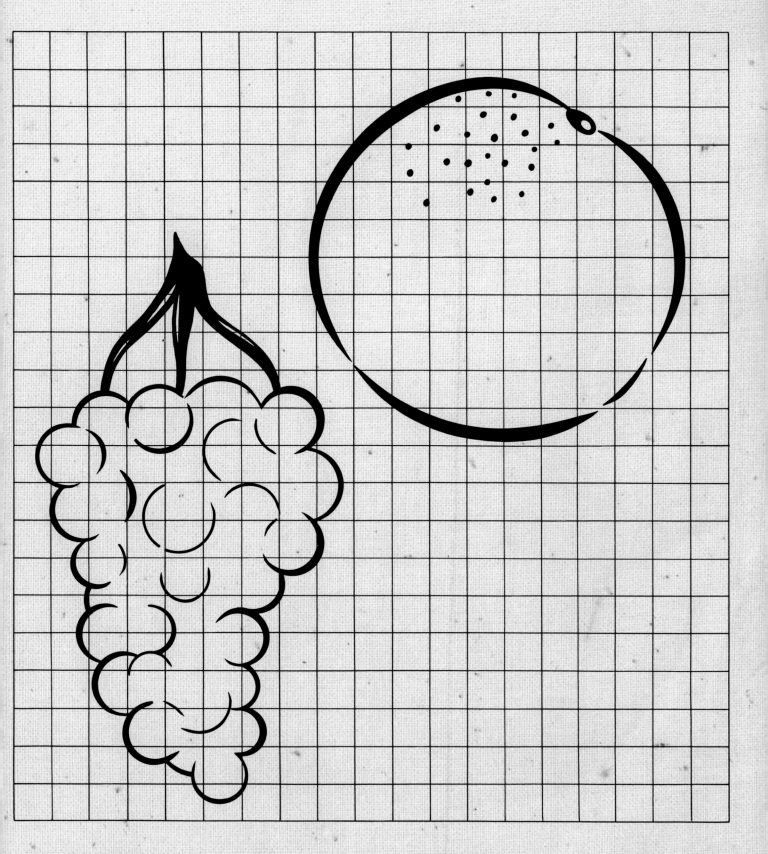

INDEX

Acknowledgments

The author would like to thank the following people and companies for their contribution:

For sharing their creative sewing and painting talents:

Christine Ben, Julia Bernstein, Millie Caltagirone, Susan Gill, Linda Heimer, Nancy Keller, Artis Nolan, Sheila Zent and the staff of Murdock Country Creations.

For the sewing notions, interfacings, fusibles, and fillers:

Dritz Corp., Freudenberg Pellon, Fairfield Processing Corp.

For the colorful trimmings, ribbon and laces:

Hollywood Trims Inc., C.M. Offray and Son Inc., William E. Wright Co., Wimpole Street Creations

For the decorative curtain rods:

Kirsch Division, Cooper Industries, Inc.

For the hand-crafted picnic basket, wooden stool, quilt rack and room divider screen:

The Longaberger Company p. 34

Walnut Hollow Farm, Inc. pp. 48, 64

For the luscious terry cloth towels and the versatile bed linens:

Dundee Mills Inc., pp. 114, 116; Wamsutta, pp. 40, 70, 112

For the beautiful fabrics which provided so much of the inspiration:

Concord Fabrics of America, pp. 32, 62

Covington Fabrics Corp., pp. 52, 56, 82, 84, 104, 108, 110, 118

Cyrus Clark Co. Inc., pp. 86, 88

Pierre Deux, pp. 30, 39, 54, 66, 88, 100, 114

Richloom Fabrics Group available at Calico Corners, pp. 50, 64, 74, 95, 96

Springs Industries, Inc., pp. 58, 76, 92

VIP Fabrics, pp. 34, 94

For providing pictures used in this book, Quarto would like to thank

Next Interiors (page 7, below) and Arthur Sanderson and Sons Ltd., London (page 8, left and page 9, right).

All other photographs are the copyright of Quarto Publishing.

We would also like to acknowledge the help of the following who kindly loaned props for the purposes of photography: the Conran Shop, London (chair, page 29); Elizabeth David Cookshop, London (copper jelly molds, page 41); The House of Steel, London (bedhead, pages 89 and 109); Next Interiors, Leicester (crook curtain rail, pages 41, 59 and 63); Purves & Purves, London (standard lamp, pages 43, 47 and 101); Villeroy and Boch, London (china, silver and glasses, page 29). Additional thanks to Judith Blacklock for her flower arrangements and Ron Carolissen for slipcovers.